Iain

Hathaway House, Book 9

Dale Mayer

Books in This Series:

Aaron, Book 1

Brock, Book 2

Cole, Book 3

Denton, Book 4

Elliot, Book 5

Finn, Book 6

Gregory, Book 7

Heath, Book 8

Iain, Book 9

Jaden, Book 10

IAIN: HATHAWAY HOUSE, BOOK 9
Dale Mayer
Valley Publishing Ltd.

ISBN-13: 978-1-773363-58-5
Print Edition

About This Book

Welcome to Hathaway House. Rehab Center. Safe Haven. Second chance at life and love.

Getting accepted to Hathaway House is the new start Iain MacLeod has been waiting for. His old VA center has put him on the road to recovery, but he's nowhere near where he wants to be. Much work remains to be done, and Iain is determined to do what's necessary to get back to full power. But he has hit the limit of his current professionals' abilities. He needs a new team. New eyes. New methods. He can only hope that Hathaway House has what he needs to keep moving forward.

Robin Carruthers works in the veterinary clinic at Hathaway House. When she connects with Iain, she's his biggest cheerleader and enjoys watching him take steps toward greater recovery. Until she realizes that, while Iain is growing in major ways, … she isn't. When traumas from her past intrude on the present, and Robin is forced to confront issues of her own, she's afraid she and Iain won't find their way back to each other again …

Sign up to be notified of all Dale's releases here!

https://smarturl.it/DaleNews

Prologue

T HE THING ABOUT change was it offered the chance for a new beginning. Iain MacLeod stared down at the acceptance letter and the rest of the papers that he had to fill out in order to make his transfer to Hathaway House happen. He took a slow and deep measured breath.

Everybody here knew him as a class clown, somebody who threw off the problems and stresses in his life without a care. Most looked at him sideways, wondering how he managed it. Only that was a facade. He knew he was at the end of his rope—that he couldn't keep it up. He knew it was time for a change, and it could only happen if he left here and went where people didn't know him. Didn't have a preconceived idea of who he was, what he was capable of doing. A place where he could go and find the depths of his soul, find a way to live with the future as he had it right now.

Because it looked pretty shitty from where he sat. He didn't want to hear any more about "probably never walk again" or "probably never be fully functioning in society again." Just so many *probably*s that he didn't even want to contemplate them.

He had both hands, and he had a sturdy back, and that was more than a lot of guys had. He was missing most of the calf on his left leg, but he still had the whole right leg. He'd taken an alternative route back to base and had driven over an IED. At least he'd been alone in the truck. So he was the only one who'd suffered. His leg had taken some of the worst of the damage. It was kind of shriveled and didn't do so well, but that's because he'd had a lot of muscle torn off it. He'd had surgeries to put new muscle back on, and, so far, it was unknown as to how well those would work. He roomed with three others, and he lived with hundreds more, all in the same nightmarish scenario that he was in. Everybody here was different, and everybody here was unique, and yet so much the same.

It hurt. All of it hurt. From his jarring life-or-death injury to the medical help to the drugs he took for the pain, but which brought other side effects to just living, sleeping, breathing, eating. It all hurt. Which was why humor had been his shield—something that might have fooled everybody else, but he knew it wasn't fooling him.

He'd gone as far as he could with his class clown skills, staring in the mirror, seeing the joker, but then acknowledging the ultimate joke which life had thrown at him. Because now he knew, if he wanted to make anything out of his world, he had to cross that abyss and had to learn to live with the best that he had, which was what that last surgery had given him.

He needed physical rehab that went well past what he had access to here, and that was stupid. This was a VA hospital. He should have had the best of the best, but he knew from what he'd seen that he didn't. At least not for himself. He knew from what he'd heard about Hathaway House that more was available there. He'd contacted several people who had been there and had come out 100 percent better. No, not perfect, not whole physically. But emotionally, spiritually and, yes, physically. All vastly improved.

They'd all told him the same thing.

"Go. You won't be disappointed."

Well, Iain had applied. He'd taken that chance, and he'd put his John Doe on an application form, then sent it off. He hadn't told anybody here, and, if he had, nobody would have been more surprised than him when he'd been accepted. Now, after more paperwork, more medical appointments, and probably a very painful transfer, then maybe he'd have a chance at a new life. Or at least a chance at living the life that he'd been given to date, as best as he could.

And really, was there more to anything in life than that?

Chapter 1

A FTER MANY DELAYS, medical appointments, measurements, and tests—more than he could even think about—Iain found himself heading toward the long driveway to Hathaway House. It wasn't the suggested ambulance transfer, as he had a friend heading back to Dallas, so he'd hitched a ride. Big mistake. The trip had been excruciating. And he wasn't at his destination yet. The VA hospital had strongly urged him not to do this, but, if he'd learned one thing in life, his stubbornness always got him what he wanted and usually with a kick in the ass to go with it.

His buddy looked at him. "You sure you want to do this?"

"We're almost there," Iain said quietly. The pain started at his back and hips. Then it filtered downward. His left leg, dear God, throbbed and burned. So did his right leg for that matter.

"You really didn't want to take an ambulance, huh?"

Iain looked at Bruce. "Would you?"

"No," Bruce said with half a smile. "I just didn't want to see you suffer."

"I don't want to suffer either," Iain said quietly, "but I didn't have too many choices."

"It's a long road trip."

"And I've spent most of it drugged out," he said.

DALE MAYER

"The VA medics said that you would suffer for this and that it would put your healing back by weeks," Bruce warned.

"Warning noted," Iain said. "I still refuse to arrive in an ambulance."

"You're stubborn," Bruce stated. When shortly thereafter he accidentally hit a pothole, it was all Iain could do to hold back his automatic moan of pain. He felt every muscle in his body tighten down, even as Bruce cried out, "Lord, I'm sorry. Hang on a minute." He dropped his speed way down. "I wasn't watching," he said. Then he glanced at Iain. "Are you okay?"

Iain slowly let out his breath, feeling his back seize like he'd never felt it before. "I will be."

"I knew this was a bad idea," Bruce said. "No point in going to a new rehab center if you're more damaged and broken than when you left the last one."

"I'll be fine," he said.

Bruce snorted. "And I'm done listening to that shit."

Iain grinned. "You're a good friend."

"Well, I understood your request," he said. "I just couldn't see somebody who's been through what you had been transferred by an ambulance."

"Exactly," he said. "And I know ... pride goes before a fall, but no way ... could I do that. It was just ... too much. Just too much on top of ... the rest," he muttered, taking shallow inhales, breathing through his nose, trying to force his body to relax. But every few seconds he froze up, expecting another lunge, another bump, and another surge of agony through his body. With relief, his gaze caught on something ahead. He reached out and grabbed Bruce's arm. "Stop for a moment."

Slowing down and then finally braking on the shoulder of the road, Bruce frowned at him. "What's up?"

And Iain pointed to Hathaway House in the distance. "I just wanted a moment to look. How often do you see something like that?" A huge estate-looking house had been built onto the hill, surrounded by green pastures, and beyond perfection in Iain's opinion.

Bruce looked at it and said, "I wish we could get out and walk around for a little bit," he said. "But I don't think that's a good idea for you, is it?"

"No," Iain said. "Definitely not." He looked at the road ahead. "It's gravel, but it's been well-graded, nicely packed, and obviously they've done a fair bit of maintenance."

"It was my fault earlier. I hit that pothole," Bruce admitted. "Like I said, I wasn't paying attention. I figured we were home free, and I eased up my guard."

"It's not your fault," Iain said and continued to stare at the huge white building ahead of him. "It's such an odd look, one-third apartment building, one-third institution, and another one-third thrown in of an old Victorian estate." He sighed, grimacing at the pain, hoping his buddy didn't see that.

Bruce pointed to the pastures all around. "Look at the pastures. Looks a bit like Kentucky, doesn't it?"

"Yeah, it does," Iain said with a smile. He caught sight of the horses in the pasture. "I know I heard about animals being here too," he said, "but I didn't realize ..."

"Horses. Wow," Bruce said, "that'll make your heart happy."

"It will," Iain said, "if I get a chance to even see them close up."

"Well, we'll find out soon," Bruce said. "You ready to

take this last step?"

"Yeah," he said. "I so am. It might be painful, and it might not be the way I thought it would work out, but I really need this change."

"Are you making it a new beginning?"

Iain smiled. "You know me too well."

"I know you were the best at making the worst situations more livable," he said. "I've been out in the trenches with you, seen you at work, cheering up the others or just distracting us from the horrors we lived through. I've been out doing routine training with you in the Middle East, near our temporary base, when we got caught in the middle of attacks, and I've seen how you somehow turned a crap deal into something that smelled like roses."

"I don't know about the roses part," Iain said with a slow smile, "but I know that I was darn glad not to be alone at those times. Thanks for sticking by me."

Bruce looked over, reached across gently, and the two gripped hands, a static handshake of sorts. "You can do this," he said.

"I know," Iain said. Then he took a deep breath. "Let's go. Let's get to this next stage of my life and whatever it'll bring."

"Stop thinking that your life is shit. It doesn't have to be. I know that Gloria walked away from your engagement because of this, but all women are not like that."

"I'm trying not to think about it," he said, "but her words are a little hard to forget."

"She had no right to say that crap," Bruce said. "You know what? Thinking of her just now, what she did to you? What she truly is?"

"Don't bother," Iain said. "I've called her worse in my

mind already. But she's right about some things. I'm not whole. I'm not 100 percent, and she's in prime breeding condition, looking for a family and somebody to be there for her. I'm hardly a good prospect anymore."

"And that's just bull," Bruce said. "If I had five minutes with that woman ..."

"You'd have sat there and stared at her in shock and not said a word," Iain said, chuckling. "Because she would have shocked the shit out of you, just like she did me. Plus, that's who you are. You'd never raise a hand to a woman any more than I would. And you know yourself that, once those nasty words leave your lips, they can never be unsaid."

"I know," Bruce said. "But, she's a piece of work." When Iain didn't respond, Bruce added, "And thankfully she's somebody else's problem. You deserve better. And Gloria had to leave your life to make room for that other woman, that better woman, that woman who was meant for you, to enter your life."

Iain sighed, gave a one-armed shrug. "Not my focus now. It's all about the rehab here."

Bruce sighed too but shot a smile his buddy's way.

They drove up the wide driveway, a massive parking lot off to one side. Bruce looked at it and said, "I'll pull up to that ramp at the front entrance, and we'll help you get up there. And then I'll come around and park."

"I'll be in the wheelchair anyway," Iain said, "so how about you just park your truck, and we'll go from there."

Bruce nodded and pulled into a parking lot not too far away. He turned off the engine and looked at his buddy and said, "I'll get the wheelchair."

"You do that," Iain said. "If I was feeling better, I'd hop out and try to make my way to the back of the truck, but today ..." He shook his head. "No, I'm not quite ready to admit this was a nasty mistake, but I am ready to accept some help."

"We all need assistance sometimes," Bruce said cheerfully. He got out, shut his driver's door, and walked to the back. He lifted the latch to the back of the truck and then dropped the tailgate. He pulled out the wheelchair and set it up.

Iain, in the meantime, shifted slowly in the front passenger seat, opened up his side door, and, with great care, made his way so he stood on the pavement. He grabbed onto the door to steady himself. He didn't have the energy to shut it. Pretty sad state of affairs.

He took a moment to focus on gathering his breath. Taking in three slow breaths, trying to get deeper each time, he calmed his racing heart and slowly let his body untense. As much as it would right now anyway. He turned, concealing the shudders running up and down his spine, knowing the painkillers had worn off hours ago. He'd been so sure he'd be okay during this trip. After all, how different would the ambulance ride be from traveling by passenger truck?

Talk about how the mighty had fallen. He took a moment, leaning against the door and just closing his eyes, taking several more deep breaths. When he could, he opened the rear side door and pulled out his bags. He dropped them on the ground, knowing he couldn't carry them anyway. He gingerly shut that door, grabbed his sunglasses from his collar, put them over his eyes, concealing the agony that resided there, and stiffened his spine.

As Bruce pushed the wheelchair toward him, the two men looked at each other. "I know this might not be the best time," Iain said, "but I really do appreciate that you've been there for me over all these years."

Bruce glared at him. "Enough of that talk. We're friends. Best friends. That's what best friends do."

Iain didn't argue, but he knew better. He'd seen many, many other men lose contact with friends and family because nobody could handle the condition they were in. He'd been blessed with Bruce. "If you want to believe that," Iain said, "I'll accept it. But I know the truth. You've gone over and above many, many times, and it's made me that much better a person."

Bruce, choking back tears, walked past his buddy and closed the front passenger door. He snagged up the two bags, tossed the big duffel over his shoulder, then plunked the other one gently in Iain's lap and said, "Let's go, buddy."

"Yeah," Iain said. "I wish I just knew to what."

"Will you be the clown here?"

"No," Iain said. "I need to walk away from that."

"You always were the darndest chameleon," Bruce said quietly. "Why the change now?"

"Because I know that something more important needs to happen here, and superficial is one thing, but I can't do that anymore. The last surgeon says the right leg is as good as it'll get. So, no more time for a facade. It's time to get real. This is all about dealing with who I am right now. It's one of the reasons I had to leave that place, as no one back there would understand the change in me or the change in what I had to do next."

"You could have done this there," Bruce muttered. "You didn't give them a chance."

"Maybe I could have, but I felt drawn to this place, so I'm willing to take the chance."

"I think that's why a lot of your buddies don't make the

change," he said. "That's why the attendance back there is so heavy. They get sucked into the same mind-set. The *this is all there is* mentality. It's because people are afraid to change."

"I've never been *afraid* of change," Iain muttered, "but I can't say I'm terribly enthralled with dealing with this one. This one came as a shock. Nobody *chooses* these kinds of monumental changes. And it takes so long just to recover enough from the last surgery to endure the next horrific surgery, which knocks you back on your ass in that hospital bed. It's a long process, and you have to remain strong throughout it all.

"And I'm probably midway in with my rehab, and I've been struggling to get through each day for the past eight months as it is. I expect it'll be another eight months here. That's why it sucks so bad when others abandon guys like me because they can't deal with the aftermath. Yet me and the others? We have no choice but to deal with the matter." He looked down at his right leg, the stronger of the two. The whole one of the two.

"You may not be happy with your physical condition yet, but Hathaway House? That's a good change. I can feel it."

As Bruce pushed him up the ramp toward the front door, Iain could only hope his friend was right and that this wasn't Iain's biggest mistake of all.

ROBIN CARRUTHERS JUST happened to be outside, taking a breather. She worked at the veterinarian floor of the Hathaway House building. She was a vet tech who had only been here a couple weeks and had already found it almost like

IAIN

home, but she was one of the few staff members here who had a residence at the center as well. She couldn't quite believe what Dani had built up here over these few short years, both on the physical property as well as the personnel. Stan, the one and only veterinarian in this place, at least for now, was a little in love with Dani but appeared more as her father figure, although he wasn't all that old. Those two had a great relationship, and, when it came to helping animals, Dani bent over backward to do anything that needed to be done.

Robin herself had considered going into veterinary school but just couldn't swing the money. She was doing so much more here than at a normal vet tech position. Primarily because they were short on hands. She shook her head. She figured she'd be doing more here anyway. It was the usual attitude at Hathaway House. Here, the people went above and beyond. Not just the staff but the patients were pleased to be here, so thankful to have such a wonderful workplace atmosphere.

She had been at other positions elsewhere, and this place topped them all. She couldn't ask for a better crew of folks to work with. Dani had employee benefits that entailed educational assistance and also allowed for educational leave for her employees too, where she would take those employees back upon completion of their studies. Not many bosses would do that for their employees. Robin sometimes wondered if she should go back to school. But, for her, she wanted more to have a husband and a family and to eventually work part-time. She wasn't as career-driven as so many other people she'd met in life. And Dani was just fine with that as well.

Robin stood here, stretching her neck and shoulders,

watching as a big black double-cab truck, heavy with chrome, but looking a little worse for wear after what could have been a long road trip, pulled into the parking lot. It was barely in her line of vision as she watched a man hop out of the driver's side and go around to the back, while the passenger, ever-so-carefully, slid his way out from the front seat. He stood shakily but on his own two feet. Then she realized that was a lie. He was standing on one foot. She was close enough to see that it hurt him to do so.

And when he closed his eyes and leaned forward to rest his head against the door, her heart went out to him. These poor guys. They were taught to man up, to not cry. Yet sometimes a good cry washed away the hurt. And, to make matters worse, these were military men. So she guessed they were too trained to hold all that pain inside, regardless. She had seen all that and more in her brother, Keith. And, with her ringside seat, she had witnessed all the pain he had to deal with from others' lack of empathy. She shook her head. *Sometimes family and friends, those closest to us, hurt us the most.*

As a vet tech, she wanted to bring some joy in the animals' lives she watched over as well as these hurting soldiers' lives. But, more than that, there was something almost spiritual about how just the presence of an animal could brighten a patient's day. She figured it was because these animals accepted us, without question. They didn't judge us, ever. They greeted people like it was the first time they had ever met, day after day. These animals, even the hurt ones down in the vet clinic, had boundless love for others.

Too bad humans weren't always like that to other humans.

Then what some humans did to animals? She shook her

head. Granted the abused animals were tough to see, and her heart went out to them each and every time, but even they rebounded and learned to love and to trust again. It was truly miraculous to watch that transformation. It gave Robin hope to deal with her own problems. Eventually.

She'd seen a lot of the patients upstairs and had some interactions with them. Not a ton, because she was so busy downstairs, but the staff brought a lot of the men and women from upstairs down to see some of the animals, and she had taken some of the animals upstairs to visit the patients.

This guy obviously was a new arrival, and not a moment too soon from the shape of him. He straightened as if he were living on guts alone.

She noted him taking what must be his last energy to put his sunglasses over his eyes. *He's hiding his pain.* Tears came to her eyes immediately.

When his buddy brought around a wheelchair and helped him into it, and when they slowly made their way to the main entrance ramp, she slid slightly out of view, so he wouldn't think that she'd been watching him at his most vulnerable moments. But this close and personal insight into the agony and the torture that these people who came here were living with? Well, that was something she generally didn't see.

She saw them at various stages of their day, sometimes with smiles on their faces and sometimes with tears drying on their cheeks. She herself was one of those people who couldn't leave anyone in pain, and it hurt her to know that so many people one floor above where she worked were suffering. But then she was working with suffering animals down below too, and it was hard. It was always hard.

Some were good stories of healing, and some were successes, but also many cases just wouldn't have a happy ending.

And she realized, not for the first time, as she watched this man slowly being wheeled up the long ramp to the front entrance reception area, that it was the same thing up above for the human patients too. She'd been so busy since her arrival here that she hadn't had time to even think about those hurting people above. She saw them almost as an auxiliary part of her job, but that human insight just now connected her in a way she hadn't expected.

She wondered who this guy was and what his story was. She could only hope that maybe Dani would make his life so much better. Of course, not just Dani but also Dani's team. And the man was in so much pain himself that Robin felt waves of it pummeling her, taking her breath away.

Yet everything that Dani had put together here was miraculous and would give this new guy hope, just like it did for the others before him. Dani and her team had replicated success after success for these military men and women. And that success had spawned the downstairs clinic.

"Robin?"

She heard Stan calling her. She peered around to see him through the window, his arms full of a gigantic rabbit. She smiled as she walked back inside to him and said, "You want me to take him?"

"Why don't you take him outside with you?" he said. "He really would like the sunshine and the green grass."

She took the massive furry bunny back out to where she'd been standing. They used a specially fenced-off yard for these rabbits because she was trying to keep the grass clean enough for the bunnies to eat it, and so she didn't want the dogs urinating here.

They had any number of different animals here that just wanted a safe place to get outside. The horses—and the llama—had the biggest fields of course, but some dogs could be allowed to roam free because they would come back with a whistle or a call. Some of the resident dogs here were housebound though, like Chickie and various other therapy animals, especially the three-legged versions. It surprised even Robin when new animals arrived who quickly became a permanent fixture here at Hathaway House.

This was a place where strays were welcomed. Robin smiled at that.

Moving into the small yard, Robin put down the big hopper. Immediately his great rounded nose twitched and trembled as he made several big hops, exploring his territory. She retraced her steps to close the four-foot gate behind her, so she could be inside with him and not have to worry about him hopping away if she turned around for a second or two. She grinned. "You look like you're doing just fine now after your surgery."

"Well, he should," Stan said. "He's healed now, so hopefully that back leg should work properly again."

She studied the bandage. "He's keeping it pretty clean. I thought he would have chewed off the bandage by now."

"I put some stuff on it to stop him from doing that."

"I've still seen them chew through that before," she said with a laugh.

Stan grinned at her. "Isn't that the truth. Where there's a will, there's a way," he said, chuckling.

She glanced back around where the ramp was to the front entrance.

"Looking for somebody?" Stan asked.

She turned and smiled up at him. "A young man just arrived," she said. "Something about the way he stood and the way he got out of the vehicle that hit close to home."

"That's right. Your brother is up here, isn't he?"

"Not yet," she said. "He's coming in about six months hopefully. He has to stabilize somewhat before he travels. Plus I don't think his bed is available until then. Even so, his arrival could be sooner or later, Dani tells me. Some of these patients leave sooner than expected, but some leave later."

"And that acceptance here, I think, is huge for his healing," he said. "Keith should do really well here."

"Well, that's one of the reasons I recommended it," she said. "In the meantime, it'll be nice to spend some time with him on a daily basis."

Stan hesitated and then said, "You know that sometimes these guys aren't the easiest to be around when they're recovering, right?"

Her smile softened. "I know," she said. "I'm not expecting miracles. But any progress would be wonderful."

Stan raised his pointer finger. "You haven't been here long enough or haven't been exposed to the human patients enough to see that miracles truly happen here." Stan nodded. "Dealing so much with the hurt animals, we don't always see what happens with their human counterparts above us. These animals are wondrous creatures. They don't realize they are missing a leg or have a cast or that half of their stomach was taken out due to cancer or a bullet wound. But our wounded warriors one floor up? Those guys and gals are dealing with some horrific hand that was dealt to them. And they have to show up every day for rehab, which is another word for *torture* in my book." Stan laughed.

"I admire each and every one of them," Robin said. "Not

sure I'd last a day. Then I catch a glimpse of someone as I get lunch two days in a row and am just amazed to see how much they have improved over the past twenty-four hours."

Stan agreed. "On the flip side, I see some backtracking, not making forward progress. Those are most likely dealing with some extra baggage on top of just their physical healing."

"Their mind-set."

"You got that right," Stan noted. "Attitude plays a big part in regaining health. Those heavy thoughts and hurtful words and just plain negative thinking can set a body back. Sometimes we humans are our own worst enemies, working against ourselves. So don't let your brother dwell on the negatives. You either," he said, wagging a finger at her, his face blooming into a full smile.

Chapter 2

"GRANTED, I MOVED here almost a month ago, so I am not able to see my brother as often as I would like to. Regardless Keith and I are close, but he has never been easy to be around," Robin said. "He's always had dark moods and a temper. But after his accident ..." She shook her head. "Nothing's been easy about it."

"And you visit him? Where he is currently?"

"At another rehab center. I saw him just before starting here," she said. "He looked like he was really struggling, suffocating in the four walls they had given him. And his progress had completely stalled."

"In that case, change is often the best answer," Stan said. He tapped her gently and pointed down at Hoppers. "What do you think?" Hoppers had made it to the far corner and was busy nibbling away on some clover in the grass.

"Seems like he'll be happy here for a while," she said. She stepped out of the fenced section with Stan, closed the gate behind them, and said, "As long as we don't leave him out too long."

"He'll be fine," Stan said. He gave the fence a shake and said, "He's not going under or over."

"He *could* go under, given enough time," she said, "but I presume this section was fenced with that in mind?"

"Yep, sure was," he said. "Chicken wire down two feet."

She groaned. "That's enough to make me cringe."

"And hopefully Hoppers too," Stan said with a chuckle. They walked back inside the vet clinic.

It was four o'clock, and they had no more scheduled patients, were down to a skeleton staff, and thus expected no more public traffic. "Are we done for the day?" she asked, reaching up a hand and rubbing her temple. "Seems like it was an extra-long day today."

"We had half the patients," he said, "but the people who came with their pets weren't necessarily the easiest."

She nodded and smiled. "The trouble is, people get just as emotionally worked up over their furry families as they do over their human families," she said. "And sometimes we just don't have answers for them."

"Sometimes I think we never have answers," Stan said soberly. "At least not the answers we want for them or that they want to hear. I've got to face a bunch of paperwork now. You want to check to make sure everybody's good for the night?"

"We're keeping three overnight, I believe?"

"Yes," he said. "I'll come in at midnight and check on them."

She nodded. "And I'll do the four o'clock check then. What about staying overnight at the clinic? Do you ever do that?"

"Way too often," he said. "But, as long as everybody handles their checks throughout the evening and night, then we can leave our patients for a few hours."

"Good." She walked into the back. A cat had had its tail run over, but the tail itself wasn't the problem. It had been pulled away from the body to a certain extent. They'd performed surgery to remove some of the remaining tailbone so the skin could close. But an injury like that often resulted in major damage internally and could affect his ability to defecate. So they were keeping a close eye on him at the moment, and he was out cold still. She checked his vitals, smiled, and moved on.

The next one was a dog who'd had a steel plate put in his back leg. He was a little bit more awake than the cat but not by much. He was also today's surgery. She bent down gently, stroked his face, and checked his vitals. She adjusted his medication and moved on to the third one, another dog who had been left intact to reproduce. He was now fixed, only he hadn't handled it well, and they were keeping him overnight because of the heavier-than-normal bleeding post-op. He appeared to be doing fine now.

That done, Robin cleaned up the back room, organizing some of the supplies that had come in.

Annette came in from the front desk and said, "I'm off, unless you need anything."

"No," Robin said with a smile. "Go have a good evening."

"Will do. See you in the morning." Annette waved, locking the main door behind her. That was the door to the public. The staff still had access to all the rest of Hathaway's yards and pool facilities—one of the huge perks of being here. Not to mention the food. She'd gained at least two pounds since she'd arrived. A pound a week didn't bode well for the end of the year. With that thought uppermost in her mind, she frowned, walked back toward Stan, and said, "Everything's cleaned up, and our three patients are doing fine for the moment. If you don't need me, I think I'll get changed and have a swim before dinner."

"Oh, that's a good idea." Stan looked up, arrested at the

thought. "I need to get back to swimming too."

"Come with me," she said. "The PT guys and gals should be done with their therapy sessions by now, shouldn't they?"

Stan checked his watch. "It's four-forty," he said. "I normally wait until five before I go in, just to make sure."

"Five would work," she said. "It'll take me a bit to walk home and get changed anyway." She stifled a yawn. "And I am tired for some reason."

"Some days are like that," he said. "I'll meet you at the pool at five then?"

She nodded, smiled, and said, "That's a deal." She headed out the back door, stopped for a moment, and realized that she'd left Hoppers outside too. She came back in and called out, "Stan, we forgot Hoppers."

He chuckled. "I was going to bring him in," he said, "but if you want to grab him ..."

She went back out to the front. There was Hoppers, stretched out on one side and enjoying the sunshine, his legs fully out in front of him. She opened the door and called him. He looked over at her, completely calm and relaxed, not otherwise responding to her call. She walked over, bent down, and picked up the big lug, cuddled him close, and then walked him back in.

Hoppers was a semipermanent resident in the place. They were trying to find a special space for him, so he could be left to roam the grounds, but his area needed to be safe. They weren't exactly sure how the new dogs would handle such a big rabbit. Would the dogs feel threatened? Would the dogs treat it as prey or food? She shuddered. She was already attached to him and surely didn't want him hurt again. While he was big enough to hold his own, the rabbit obviously had no defenses against an attack, like maybe another pet would.

She put him back into his large glassed-in space, with plenty of air holes for ventilation and a strong wire gate atop, where they kept him overnight inside the vet clinic. He immediately headed off to his sawdust and curled up, as if to go to sleep. She closed the door to Hoppers' cage and said to Stan, "He's back in his space. I sure hope we can get him an outdoor yard, where we can leave him outdoors a little more often."

"And probably we could leave him overnight in the yard he just came out of," Stan said.

She nodded and said, "Maybe, but I feel better having him inside. I'll meet you in a few minutes at the pool." And she headed off to her on-site apartment. She smiled at the thought. She had been very lucky to land this job and even more so to have free room and board added in as huge perks on top of her generous salary.

Nothing like a swim at the end of the long day, especially in a place like this. She couldn't wait until her brother arrived. And maybe, just maybe, they could move past all the problems that they had themselves. They would definitely have more time together to work through those. And face-to-face. *That had to be better, right?*

After all, nobody here was problem-free, including her.

IAIN SAT ON the bed, almost in too much pain to even hear the words from the owner-manager of the place. Dani reached out and in a firm voice said, "Lie back down again." He looked at her, wanting to glare at the woman, but he didn't have the strength. She just gave him a clipped shake of her head. He eased back down and closed his eyes, feeling the trembling running throughout his body. That was never a good sign. Of course he knew what it meant. *You've overdone it. Again. You've got to learn to ask for help.*

"I understand that you came by truck," she said, "and I get that. You're not the first one. You won't be the last one either, no matter how we try to talk you military guys out of this. But I can tell you that it sets you back at least a day or two. Maybe more. That's for your doctors and your PT specialist to determine. Now, if you just relax and don't do a whole lot for the next couple days, we should be able to minimize the damage."

He opened his eyes and looked at her. "I just couldn't stomach the idea of arriving by ambulance."

"I get it," she said softly. "I do."

And, from her tone, he believed her. He smiled. "You've seen everything, haven't you?"

"Well, I think so," she said cheerfully. "And then somebody does something that surprises me." She handed him an Apple tablet and, pointing, said, "Besides your mandated bed rest, for the remainder of today, you'll need to go over paperwork, and your team and others will come in here to visit and to talk with you. Your schedule is in the tablet too. But I'll start first with one of your doctors and some pain meds."

"I still have a few," he said. "They're in my pocket. I can take those now and then later, when the doctor has a chance to assess my condition."

"That's fine," she said, "as long as they are standard-issue."

He grinned. "Yes." He pulled them out of his pocket,

shifting with a little bit of awkwardness. "This is all they are." And he handed her the medicine bottle.

She looked at him, studied the label, opened the bottle, checked that the inside matched the outside, and nodded. "Okay. I'll get you some water," she said, walking into his en suite bathroom. When she returned and watched him take two of his pills, she added, "I'll go get your doctor now." As she walked to the doorway, she turned. "In the meantime, take a look at what I've given you."

As she walked out, he flicked through the tablet, amazed at the technological level at which they were operating, but he realized, of course, it was necessary in today's day and age. His body was still on fire, but the fact that he was in a bed had taken the pressure off his spine, and the rest of him was holding. He kept telling himself that he had a strong back, but he kept putting it under so much physical strain and stress that he wondered if his back was still strong enough.

He looked at the data regarding the members of his medical team and who had been assigned to him, but none of the names meant anything to him. He had a doctor, two nurses, a therapist, and a psychologist. At that, he frowned.

Dani walked back in and asked, "What's the frown for?"

"Psychologist?"

"Everyone here sees a psychologist," she said. "Him or her, we have two on staff."

He looked up at Dani. "And how often?" He hated how that little bit of suspicion was evident in the back of his voice, but, of all the medical professionals Iain didn't trust, they had to be at the top of the list. Something was just so off-putting about knowing that people were trying to read something into or glean something from every word he said, and that made him not want to say anything.

She smiled. "We'll start with once every couple days, until the doc has a chance to assess your condition. Then it'll ease back to once a week, maybe once every couple weeks," she said cheerfully. "As long as you're making progress, as in you're doing well emotionally, as in you're stable and sound, then there's no reason to suspect you need more than that."

He winced. "You'll really put me through it, won't you?"

"I so am," she said. "Remember. You came here for the whole package, not a partial job."

"And if I want to change my mind?"

She laughed, and he knew that she hadn't taken him seriously.

"I get that," she said, "and I understand. But that time's past. It's a whole different story though, now that you're actually here."

"I guess," he said, giving in. "It's just weird to think of anybody poking around in my brain."

"No, that's the brain surgeon," she said. "These guys poke around in your mind."

He just glared at her, and she laughed. "Now I've already given you the rules, and I've told you all about how the system works. It's after five, but you are not coming down to the cafeteria for dinner tonight," she said.

His frown deepened. "And yet I'm hungry," he said, worried he'd miss dinner.

"Good," she said. "I will take it upon myself to see what's for dinner. I'll come back and give you an idea of the choices, so you can tell me what you want."

His eyebrows rose in surprise. "Don't you have better things to do than look after me?"

She stopped midway to the door. She turned and looked at him and said in a very calm, quiet voice, "I have nothing better to do than to look after you and every other patient in this building." And, on that note, she walked out the doorway.

He laid here in bed, listening to her as she walked down the hallway, her strides casual yet determined. He realized then what was unique about being here. He'd never felt like he'd mattered to anybody else in any of the other centers he'd been to. He had always been just a number, and every number meant more money to the institution.

Obviously it meant more money here too, but he never had that same heartfelt reaction, that sense of belonging, or that the sense of being someone who mattered. He took a long, slow breath and let it out. Then he picked up his phone and sent Bruce a message. **Thanks again for bringing me here**, he texted. **I can't go to dinner myself, but they'll bring me something, and I've been put on bed rest to recover from my travels.**

Bruce answered almost immediately but this time with a phone call. "Are you okay?" Bruce asked. "I didn't want to leave you there, but it seemed like I was in the way."

"You couldn't stay at that point, but you do get to come back, if you're around and available for a visit," he said.

"I'll do that," he said. "You know I'm gone for the next ten days anyway. But after that ..."

"Hopefully after that, I'll have moved on and forgotten that lovely drive. Especially that pothole," he said with a short laugh.

"You would be the one to remind me of that," Bruce said with a chuckle.

"Well, I just wanted to say *thank you* again," Iain said. "I know you've got to get home and to get ready for your trip, but I wanted you to know that I'm fine."

"That's all right," he said. "We're living and breathing change right now for both of us."

"Exactly." Iain knew his friend had just separated from his wife and was still trying to patch things up. They were doing a trip to sort things out and to see if they could make it work. "Good luck on your trip. You know I wish you the best."

"Yeah," Bruce said. "You know I care about you too, buddy. You continue to do the best you can, and I'll be there for you." And he hung up.

Caught up with emotions, he wanted to send Bruce's wife a message and tell her what a great guy she had, if she'd only smarten up and find a way to figure that out. Then Iain realized it wasn't his job. No matter how much Bruce might have told him, his wife hadn't told her side of the story. And it just wasn't Iain's place. He really liked Laura too. But it was up to them to work it out, not Iain.

Just then he heard footsteps nearing his door. Dani walked in, a piece of paper in her hand. She held it out and said, "We'll try and get the cafeteria guys to post the menus online sometime soon. It would save trips like this."

"Trips like this?" He reached for the piece of paper and smiled. "Seriously, you're having a Mexican night?"

"For those who like Mexican food, but other options are offered as well."

"I love Mexican food. And, if you've got enchiladas, I would be happy to have some."

"You'll need your plate one-quarter full of vegetables too," she said. "We don't chintz in the food department, and we expect nutrition to be a high priority."

He raised his eyebrows. "I love vegetables," he said mildly. "So either a plate of hot vegetables or a big salad on the side would be fine."

"When you say big …?"

He smiled, held up his hands in a circle, like for a midsize bowl, and said, "I don't know how much I can eat after that trip, but I am hungry, and it seems like I could use a good-size bowl."

"Good. I'll send Dennis down in a little bit when he catches a break at the line," she said. "He'll introduce himself. He runs the cafeteria. So, anything you want, you can have."

"Perfect," he said in surprise. He settled back against the bed, just happy to have his muscles relaxing a little bit.

"And one of your medical doctors will be in fairly quickly," she said. "He wants to check you over and see how those muscle relaxants are working." As she stopped in the doorway, she smiled at someone down the hallway and said, "Dr. Burgess is here now."

Iain could feel himself tensing before the older gray-haired man in a white lab coat stepped in. But his smile and friendliness were sincere and caring. At that, Iain relaxed, knowing that, although he might be in trouble for pushing his body too far today, he didn't think Dr. Burgess would interrogate him.

Chapter 3

SEVERAL DAYS LATER, the man she'd seen arrive crossed Robin's path again. She was walking around the ground floor with one of the big new cats in her arms. This one was missing a leg, but his temperament was being tried out as a therapy cat. The staff had found that having the formerly injured animals around gave the human patients in the facility additional hope and that they would bond in some way, furthering their rehab efforts.

So, this was Max. He had a patch of fur missing off his hip that had refused to grow back, but apparently he was doing much better. He was mobile—a little too mobile to be let loose right now—and happy, and, as soon as you even looked at him, that diesel engine of his kicked in. She was going from room to room, asking the human patients on the floor above the vet clinic if they wanted to say hi. She hadn't met anyone saying no yet. Even those with that initial *stay away from me* vibe instantly broke into a big grin, their walls completely down. It was amazing to watch, each and every time.

As she approached the next room, the door was open, so she stuck her head in and said, "Hey."

A man looked up, and she was surprised to see who it was. The new arrival she had seen. She smiled and said, "I have Max here, if you'd like to say hello."

He looked at her in surprise, then at the cat in her arms. "Wow," he said, "can you actually carry that thing?"

"He is on the heavier side of twenty pounds," she said, "so part of his rehab includes losing weight." She walked in, held Max out, then placed him gently on the bed.

The patient looked at her—held his gaze there for quite a while—smiled, and said, "I don't think I've seen you around here before." He reached out a hand. "I'm Iain. I arrived a few days ago."

She nodded. "I'm Robin. I'm one of the vet techs downstairs."

He grinned. "Well, that explains why I haven't seen you." He reached down to pet Max. "Wow, look at this guy." Max immediately walked up his chest and butted him in the head. Iain chuckled. He wrapped his arms around the cat and said, "The advantage of a cat being this big is you can really hug them," and he held Max close for a moment, just letting his face rest against the big cat's head. Max took it for a long time. "His temperament is beautiful," he muttered.

She smiled and reached down to pat Max. "We're testing him out as a possible therapy cat," she murmured.

He looked at her with interest.

She shrugged. "We work with a society in town, and they work with animals that can go to children's wards in hospitals and also to visit with terminal patients—difficult cases where anything like this might put a smile on their faces."

"I love hearing that," he said warmly.

She studied him, her smile growing bigger. "Besides, Max put a smile on your face, didn't he?"

He winced. "Yeah. … Did it look like I wasn't too happy with life when you first came in?"

"Not so much," she said. "But it's obvious you're not lying here relaxed and comfortable."

He looked at her in surprise.

She shrugged. "I deal with animals all the time. Humans are just bigger animals."

"That's the truth," he said. "Sometimes we're easy to deal with, and sometimes we're not."

"The same for all animals," she said.

Max, not liking to be ignored, immediately head-butted Iain again. He chuckled and scratched the big guy under his chin. "He looks like a tabby with those big rings, but he's so much larger."

"We're not exactly sure what other breed is in Max," she said, "but his previous owners had him declawed, and that's not a good idea when around other animals and, of course, never when outside. They have no way to defend themselves if they are attacked."

"Well, as a therapy cat," he said, "it would probably be okay."

"Well, for the moment, I'm mostly carrying him around, or he would get away from me really quick," she said. "I'll have to get him used to a harness though, for that kind of therapy work."

"That should be fun," he said, laughing. "Anytime anybody needs a chuckle, you should grab a group of us and put the harness on Max in front of us all, so we can watch this guy get out of it in two seconds flat."

She grinned, loving his humor. "Are you settling in okay?"

The smile fell off his face, and he nodded. "Yeah. I had a rough arrival," he said.

"You're not the only one to say that," she said. Max stood up and walked down to the end of the bed, sprawling down where Iain's left leg ended. She walked over to him, picked him up in her arms, and said, "I'll take him to visit somebody else now." She walked to the door and smiled at Iain. "Take it easy."

"You too," he said with a lingering smile.

IAIN WAS INCREDIBLY surprised by the visit but was also heartened by it. Robin, … well, she radiated warmth. A special kind that he was not used to. And Max? He laughed at the thought. Robin and Max's visit highlighted how different Hathaway House was. Yet again. One of the things that he missed in his life was not having pets. He'd been raised in a family with lots of kids and lots of animals. Only his human family remained, but nobody knew how to deal with him right now. He'd given them the same joker personality treatment, but they'd already known that was the fake Iain, and so he'd avoided them at all costs, since they kept asking him questions he would rather not answer. He should have taken a picture of Max to send to them, as they would have understood Iain's joy in seeing and holding a pet again.

Only they would have also seen that he was in bed still, with a sheet over his legs. *Leg*, he kept reminding himself. He had one, the whole right leg now. He took a deep breath and reminded himself that he *had* one leg and that he should be grateful to have that. How it had been touch-and-go and how he could have lost that one too. Something he didn't really want to focus on. For that matter, he had to be grateful that he had like 75 percent of his left leg.

As he relaxed here, he looked up to see Shane, standing at the doorway, studying him for a long moment. Of course they had met on his first day here, but Iain's full medical team soon found out he was in no shape to start his recommended PT rehab plan. Not yet. And he wouldn't recover in two days' time either, despite what Dani had said initially. That may have worked with the others before Iain, but he had really done a number on himself this time.

Shane asked, "So, on a scale of one to ten, how's the body?"

"Three."

"Right. That trip of yours caused some inflammation and swelling on your spine," he said. "Plus the leg joint is not too happy. I was thinking about the pool or hot tub to ease the swelling a bit. What's your preference?"

"Either would be great," Iain said instantly. "I figured the pool and the hot tub were rewards for after I'd done some hard work, not after a mistake like this."

"I think just getting you down there and getting you mobile in the water, where we can get some of the joints moving without any weight on them, would be a good place to start," he said. "Do you have swimming trunks?"

With dismay, Iain shook his head. "No, I don't. I didn't really consider the pool as an option for me."

"I'll be back," Shane said, and he smacked the door and left.

Iain didn't know if that meant that shorts were available or what Shane would do, but Iain really didn't want to lose out on an opportunity to get into the water if he could. And Shane was right. The inflammation was worse—seems no movement was not good, although too much movement was definitely bad—but Iain had been trying to minimize it with heat and ice and anti-inflammatories.

Of course he almost reverted back to that old joker personality of his, where he would laugh it off. Instead, he should have been open in acknowledging it and asking for help. But some here had seen it immediately. He wondered if Robin had said something because she'd been the last one he'd seen. He frowned, wondering about that insightful part of her, wondering if she saw enough—or too much—and then realized it didn't matter if it had been her or not. He was grateful that somebody had noticed because he himself hadn't.

Shane returned about fifteen minutes later, holding up two pairs of trunks. "Different sizes," he said, "let's see which one we can get you in and out of the easiest. After swiveling his legs to the side and pushing the sheet back, he allowed Shane to help him get dressed and then into a wheelchair.

"Well, I'm glad the first pair fit," Iain said, gasping for breath. "I didn't realize how much the movement would hurt."

"And that's something you've got to keep an eye on," Shane said quietly. "No strong silent types needed, please. We've got enough of those around here. Take an interest in your own healing and be active in your own treatment."

"I hear you," Iain said, "but I might need a few reminders."

"Not a problem," Shane said cheerfully. "I've got no problem doing that for you, particularly if I see that you're showing some progress. What pisses me off is when I see guys with potential who won't apply themselves."

"Do you get many of those?"

"Too many," he said, "but not for long."

"Meaning, you ship them out?" And that was the last thing he wanted to hear.

"No," Shane said. "I definitely don't ship them out," he said with a laugh. "But we do shift that attitude real fast."

Chapter 4

R OBIN STEPPED OUTSIDE with a cup of coffee in her
hand and brushed the hair off her face. She could hear
several men laughing and joking nearby. *Happy humans
nearby*, she thought with a smile. That was the thing down
here. Happy animals made happy sounds, like barks, purring
engines, but too often in a place like this they were silent or
resorted to aggressive barking because the animals didn't
want to be here. Like now. They'd just finished a tough
surgery, and she could use the break. Stan came out beside
her with a cup of coffee in his hand. The two looked at each
other and smiled.

"It went well," Stan said. He motioned at the sun chairs
out in the front. "Let's sit down and relax for a minute."

She walked with him over to the side and realized that
they were approaching the patio where the pool was. "Is it
okay to sit here when the patients are outside?"

"Absolutely," he said. "The more we intermingle, the
better. It stops the alienation and that line between *them and
us.*"

It made sense, and she was happy to collapse for a moment. "That Jack Russell," she said and then stopped and
shook her head, "I thought we would have to put him
down."

"We might still," Stan said, leaning his head back, his

41

face up to the sun. He took a deep slow breath and let it out. "But, with any luck, he'll pull through."

"I can't stand to see anyone in pain," she murmured. Her gaze swept to the side, where at least six men had gathered in the pool, some doing laps and some doing what looked like PT exercises. Two men were in the hot tub. No females were around at the moment. And just then, two women came, both in shorts and T-shirts with clipboards in their hands, so they were probably therapists. Robin smiled as she watched the men get put through the paces. And then she recognized one in the hot tub was Iain.

Stan, his voice low, commented, "Anyone you fancy?"

She snorted. "It's been a long time."

"It doesn't matter how long it's been," he said. "When there's a spark, there's a spark."

She smiled, nodded, and said, "True enough. But I haven't been here long enough."

"Liar," he said with a chuckle.

She grinned. "What about you?" she asked. "Anybody here for you?"

"No, I haven't had a serious relationship in over a year," Stan said. "I'm wed to my work."

"I hear you," she said. "It doesn't change the fact that, when it happens, it happens, but you have to be in a position where you can meet people so it can happen."

He burst out laughing. "Good point," he said. "I thought maybe somebody would be here for me over time, but, so far, it hasn't happened." He shifted comfortably, then lifted his coffee and took a sip. "Man," he said. "My lower back is killing me. I have to get that height adjustment fixed on the surgical table."

"Yeah, that mechanism needs to be repaired," she murmured. "That awkward bending we did today was due totally to the wrong height."

"I'll make sure somebody calls about it this afternoon."

"If I get a chance, I will," she said. "I know we don't have long to enjoy these five minutes because the appointments are starting this afternoon, but, boy, oh, boy, it got busy this morning."

Stan grunted his agreement.

She smiled as she watched Iain in the hot tub, and then Shane approached him, and Iain slid up and over and, rather than standing, he shuffled on his butt over to the pool before sliding in. She could see his left leg missing most of the calf, and his right leg—from where she sat—was purple and angry and about half the size it should be. She winced.

"Looks pretty raw, doesn't it?" Stan asked beside her.

She rolled her head toward him, her eyes welling. "God," she said. "What he must have gone through."

Stan studied him, but she didn't dare turn and look back.

"What he's *still* going through," Stan murmured. "He's got to build that muscle back up. It looks like some of it has been surgically reattached. It'll take a lot of time and effort."

She nodded. "It'll be worth it though," she said, "because that'll give him one good leg. Presumably at that point he might have a prosthetic for the other."

"I think so, but it depends on the damage. I've put prosthetics on many animals, and sometimes it's for the good, and sometimes the animal was better off without it."

She smiled. "I think it's all about adaptation. Speaking of which," she said, standing. "We have to adapt to the fact that our break time is over."

He groaned. "You are a slave driver."

"If you won't get help in," she said, "we pretty well have to be our own slave drivers."

"Aaron is coming," he said. "Just can't happen fast enough."

"He's also pretty green, right?" she warned.

"True, but he's gifted," Stan said. "I'd be more than happy to have him join in."

"Good to know," she said. She walked back with him and said, "Do you want to bet we have twenty people in the waiting room?"

"I hope not," he said. They opened the door, and she laughed.

"Maybe not twenty," she said, "but at least a dozen."

He groaned, and they both walked in with smiles on their faces and got back to work.

IAIN LOOKED AT the calendar in shock. It had been two weeks. Two weeks, when it seemed like he'd arrived yesterday. It had taken much longer than two days to get over the inflammation from his long truck drive, and he still hadn't seen Bruce. He was due back in another couple days, having delayed his return for whatever reason. Iain hadn't heard from his buddy yet.

As he got dressed this morning, Iain realized that, so far, everything had been pretty easy and smooth. They were proceeding based on what his body could handle, and he appreciated that. But he also had the sense of not making any progress. When he looked back to where he'd come from two weeks ago, he realized his progress so far was basically getting back to normal, getting back to where he'd been.

How depressing was that? The knock on the door brought him out of his musings and back to the present.

Fully dressed, he looked up and called out, "Come in." He was surprised to see the woman who had brought Max the cat last time. He raised his eyebrows.

She smiled and said, "I know you're heading out for the morning, but I was just wondering if you wanted to say hi to somebody."

"Sure. What somebody is this?"

She opened the door wider but didn't step closer. She held a leash in her hand.

"Did Max finally learn to wear a harness?"

She chuckled. "No, Max is still a project in the making," she said. "Come on, Hoppers." She pushed the door open more and in hopped one of the biggest, fluffiest rabbits he'd ever seen in his life.

He stared in shock. "Did you feed that thing steroids?"

She smiled. "He's a giant breed," she said, as she bent down, scooped him in her arms, and brought him over, closer to Iain.

Instantly the rabbit leaned forward, his nose twitching and his whiskers wiggling as he tried to sniff Iain.

He reached up a hand, gently stroking the bunny's face and his long soft ears. "He's adorable," he said warmly. He shook his head. "You know what? I kind of like your job."

"You do when it's nice," she said with a smile, reaching down to kiss Hoppers, still in her arms. "But parts of it aren't so nice."

He nodded soberly. "I can imagine." He scratched and played with Hoppers's big ears, admiring his legs. "Will he be another therapy animal?"

"Could be. He basically lives here now," she said. "It's

good for him and for you guys to see him and visit with him. We're hoping to build him a little pen, that he can come and go from, on a regular basis, which will allow him to spend a few hours outside without us."

"That's a good idea," he said. "Wish I was back on my feet. I used to be pretty handy at building that kind of stuff."

"Well, as soon as you're mobile, we could use your help," she said, holding out the rabbit again.

Iain reached out automatically, and, when Hoppers landed full weight in his arm, he *oof*ed. "Wow," he said. "This guy and Max are a mated pair."

She burst out laughing. "He's got some heft to him, doesn't he?"

"Amazing," he said. In awe, he reached down toward his face and his smooth silky neck. "He's beautiful. Do you think the clinic would mind if I putted around with a hammer and some nails?"

"No, I don't think they'd mind in the least," she said. "You'd have to clear whatever project you envisioned with Dani and your medical team, but, other than that, I'm sure they're happy to have some free labor."

"Maybe, depends if I can get clearance from Shane."

"That'll be a challenge." She grinned. "Now you can have your breakfast. I just wanted you to meet Hoppers." She scooped him back out of his arms and walked away.

He studied her as she left, wishing he had a reason to call her back. "Robin?"

She stopped at the doorway, then turned toward him with one eyebrow up. "What's up?"

He shrugged and said, "Nah, it's okay."

She frowned deeper. "Well, it's not okay," she said. "You did call me."

He shrugged. "I just wondered if there was a way for people to get up and out of here too into the pastures, like the rabbit? If I ever get *peopled out*?"

Her initial confusion cleared. "You mean, like wanting to head down to the pastures to spend some time over in our corner of the woods instead of here?"

He nodded. That was close. It wasn't quite what he wanted to say, but it headed in the right direction. "Something like that," he said with a shrug. "It'd be nice to sit down, have a coffee with somebody, and get to know them, instead of being surrounded by hundreds of somebodies."

She grinned, surprised and flattered to think that he wanted to have coffee with her. "My break is at noon," she said. "I plan on sitting out in the pasture, so feel free to join me if you want, and I'll introduce you to the horses."

"I miss horses," he said in a low voice.

"Are you used to horses?"

He nodded. "Yeah, I am," he said. "I've been riding ever since I was a kid." He looked down at his mangled right leg, and his left leg missing its foot and beyond and said, "Make that past tense."

"Doesn't have to be," she said. "We have horse therapy here on a weekly basis." She frowned. "Didn't you know about that?"

He looked at her, shook his head slowly, and said, "No, I hadn't heard about that. I knew horses were here ..."

"Mention it to Shane," she said. "He may not think that you're quite ready yet, but it's an option down the road. And, if you're a good rider, we have lots of other people here who ride horses. I think you have to talk to Dani about that though, because she handles all the horses."

"Well, Dani is right here," Dani said, interrupting the

two. She stepped into Iain's room and looked at them. "I just happened to be walking down the hallway. What's up?"

"He was wondering what the horse therapy thing was," she said. "He's used to being around horses, been riding forever."

Dani looked at him with a smile. "And, if you're a horse person," she said, "it's got to be hard not to have them close by again."

"It is," Iain admitted. "Just seeing them outside again is pretty special."

"So true," Dani said. "I'll see when the next opening is in the horse therapy, but I guess we must get clearance from Shane first."

"Shane," Iain said with a shake of his head. "It sounds like he's the go-to man in this case."

"We use horseback riding as therapy, and it's a recurring thing here. So if you miss the next session—or four—you'll catch it later," Dani said seriously. "And, if it's the right thing for you, then that's perfect. But, if it will hinder your healing, it's not a good thing."

"Right," he said. "That makes sense."

"Absolutely, but I have seen you in the hot tub already, so Shane must be thinking of moving you to the pool. That's something you can look forward to as well," Dani said with a smile. "Is that okay with you?"

He thought about it, realized that Shane had been the one who had been here every day for him so far, and he nodded. "Shane is a good guy," he said with a smile. "And, speaking of which, I need to get moving so I'm not late for my appointment with him."

"Never do that," Dani warned. "He doesn't like slackers."

"So far I don't feel like I've been doing very much," he said drily. "Slacking just seems to be the way of it here. I expected much more."

Dani looked at him in surprise for a moment. Then she nodded. "I think your arrival slowed things down."

"Well, I'm ready to have that slowness taken off my chart and make some progress," he announced.

She smirked. "Watch what you say. You could come back to your room today feeling very sorry to have spoken those words."

"Maybe," he said with a shrug. "But it's better to feel like you're doing something and feeling the pain of it than to be doing nothing and feeling nothing rewarding either."

"Then tell Shane that," Dani said. "There's lots you can do once you reach this point, you and your body."

"Will do."

Chapter 5

ROBIN WONDERED OVER the next few days how Iain had done with Shane *unleashed*. She'd gone out to lunch that afternoon, as she had mentioned to Iain, thinking he would join her, but Iain hadn't shown up. She'd gone out a few days later, and again she saw no sign of him. Now she stopped expecting him to show up at lunch, thinking that either something must have happened or he hadn't been quite so ready to make that lunch date with her. He'd seemed to be the one making that initial gesture, but maybe his health hadn't been as strong as he'd hoped.

Still, she didn't want to go to his room and make it seem like she was pushing him. It was dinnertime on Friday, her last day before two days off, and she walked upstairs after a shower. It had been another tough day with so many people in the clinic. It wasn't a surgery day thankfully, but lots of individuals were picking up animals, so it seemed like a never-ending revolving door of activity today. As she walked toward the cafeteria, she saw Stan at the top of the stairs, waiting for her. "You ready for dinner?"

He nodded. "I was thinking about taking mine and going back to my apartment," he said. There was such exhaustion in his expression, and the lines on his face etched a little deeper.

"I hear you," she murmured. "I just figured I'd sit in the

sun and soak up some of that late afternoon heat."

"Don't burn," he warned.

"Nope, I won't," she said.

They separated at the line as Stan got his to go. He must have arranged it ahead of time because he ended up getting a tray with silver domes on top. He smiled at her as he disappeared back down the stairs.

She got into line, and Dennis looked at her and said, "You look as bad as he does."

She wrinkled her nose up at him. "Okay, now that sounds pretty bad."

Dennis went off on peals of laughter. "Vegetables," he said. "That'll help perk you up. You need nutrition."

"And I love my sautéed vegetables," she said, "but I was thinking something like a big salad first."

"How about a big chef's salad?"

"Or a cobb salad?"

"You pick," he said. "Happy to make it for you."

"How about a chef's salad with some fried chicken on the side," she said, when staring at some in front of her.

He chuckled. "What is it about fried chicken that gets everybody every time?" he asked with a big smile.

A voice beside her said, "And here I thought it was just me."

Startled, she looked over to see Iain, standing on crutches. He towered above her.

"Wow," she said. "I knew you were tall, but I didn't realize how tall."

He grinned down at her. "I'd probably still be taller than you, even if I stood on my stump."

She shook her head and grinned. "Can you get a prosthetic for that?" She motioned to his missing foot and calf.

"Working on it," he said easily. He hobbled forward as she moved her tray down.

Dennis looked at him, grinned, and said, "Man, I like to see you on your feet."

"Me too," he said. "Whatever you're making for her, make one for me too, will you?"

"Supersize it though?"

"I can get behind that," Iain said.

She laughed. "What if you don't like what I'm having?"

"He was talking veggies and nutrition," Iain said. "That's something I definitely need to focus on."

She nodded. "I guess what you put in your body is just as important as the rehab work you do, isn't it?"

"Absolutely it is," Dennis interrupted, not giving Iain a chance to respond. "You guys go pick your places. I'll come and deliver."

"Are you sure?" she asked, frowning at him.

"Of course I'm sure," he said.

"Okay," she said. "I just don't want to add to your workload."

"And I thank you for that." Dennis beamed. "But this is a pleasure. Go find a table, and I'll bring it."

She walked forward, slipping out of the line and heading toward the juices and water section. Iain was right on her heels. She pointed to what was in front of them and said, "I want just water but maybe coffee afterward."

"That's a good idea," he said. "I think I'll have some milk to go with mine."

She nodded. And, not giving him a chance, she grabbed one of the bottles of milk for him and a bottled water for her, then asked, "Anything else?" With both on her tray, she snatched up the cutlery they needed and said, "I might as well carry it. It's not like we both need to."

"That's a good idea. I'm not great at walking with crutches and also carrying trays yet," he said with a smile. "I've seen lots of guys do it though."

"Come on. Let's go find a place to sit," she said. "Inside or outside?"

He hesitated. "You know what? I'd like to do outside, but I'm afraid it'll be deadly hot, so how about half and half?" He pointed at a table with the shade line down the center.

She chuckled. "That's perfect because I was thinking I'd like to sit in the sunshine." As they made their way to the table, she didn't offer to help him navigate. Something she'd been warned about when she first started working downstairs was to make sure the patients didn't think that she was pitying them or taking it easy on them, pride being a very subtle and sensitive yet critical issue. After they sat, and she opened her bottle of water, she took a drink, smiled at him, and said, "How are you adjusting?"

"Well, I'm adjusting," he said. "Not terribly fast though."

She waited for him to continue that thought.

"I told Shane a few days ago that I was ready for more, but, after a test run—which is why I missed lunch with you that day—he thought I needed another week, to get the inflammation down more. So, I'm still waiting."

She nodded. "Any other surprises?"

He hesitated.

She lifted her eyebrows and said," You can talk to me, you know?"

"Can I?" The corner of his mouth quirked.

"Yep," she said. "When I moved here, I found it difficult

to adjust myself."

"Adjust to what?"

"The multiple changes in my life. Change from a big city to this. Change from having a relationship to not. Change from my previous job to this new one. I had a lot of adjustments, and I decided to make it a new beginning for myself. But, as such, I didn't have any foundation or any history to go on here. Nothing to draw on in my experiences to make it easier."

He cocked his head to the side as he studied her.

She gave a self-conscious shrug. "I guess that doesn't make a whole lot of sense, does it?"

"It makes more sense than you realize," he said slowly. "At the VA hospital where I was, I was the class clown. I was joking and laughing, and I knew that it was just a facade and that underneath nobody could really see the pain I was in. I promised myself I wouldn't do that when I got here."

"I like the sound of that," she said. "Because, of course, the class clown is hiding something. It's usually pain or embarrassment or lack of confidence."

He smiled. "In my case it was the inability to deal with the body that I currently live in. I kept hoping and hoping that the surgeries would work. And, of course, the jury is still out as to whether they really will."

"You're walking," she said slowly. "In my book, that's a huge success."

He looked at her, startled, and then he nodded. "And that's what I just came to realize," he said. "When I left that place and came here, I was determined to find out who I really am. I want to be who I am on the inside, not just the person on the outside everybody saw."

"And that sounds very deep too. I think, when you get

an opportunity to be at a place like this," she said slowly, "you almost have to wipe out everything that came before. You can challenge the good things, the things that worked, taking them to a new level. Things that pissed you off from the old life almost have to be put in a box and stowed away, so you can give this experience a chance, without that prior stuff hindering your vision. A fresh start to take each new experience from a whole new perspective."

"Easier said than done," he said with a smile.

"I'm just as guilty. I came with what I thought was a broken heart, only to realize very quickly that I wasn't brokenhearted. It was more like a dent to my pride," she said with a self-deprecating smile. She lifted her water bottle and took another big sip. "My heart wasn't touched. My pride took a blow when I realized he preferred somebody else to me."

"I'm sorry," he said.

She shook her head. "I'm not," she said. "The best thing I did was come here. If I had stayed with him and had tried to make it work, we both would have been unhappy. Where's the joy in that?"

He gave a shout of laughter. "A perfect way to look at it," he said. "I'm trying to take this as a new experience and come to terms with who and what I am right now."

"What you are," she said firmly, "is a man with a disability. But you are not a disabled man. Those are two very different things."

He stared at her in surprise. "I think I like that," he said slowly.

She nodded. "It's all about perspective," she said. "What you've already done since you've been here is great."

"No, right there, you're wrong," he said. "I haven't done

anything yet. I don't even feel like I've had to apply myself."

"Maybe the harder thing for you was to do nothing," she said seriously. "You came here in bad shape. You were ready to do the old gung-ho, charge-forward thing. But instead, what you had to do first was ease back, relax, and let your body destress and deal with the extra damage because of that trip."

He glanced at the table. "Maybe," he said. "I'm not very good at doing nothing."

"And, after two—now three—weeks of doing nothing, as you say, you're feeling like you haven't made any progress. Yet it's the opposite. You should be slowly improving to the point that now maybe you can get to work. The real work you came here for."

Just then Dennis arrived, carrying large plates of food. He placed them on the table, stepped back, then looked at them both expectantly.

She smiled up at him. "Thank you. It looks lovely."

"And," Dennis said with a huge toothy grin, "it tastes even better. I'll be back in a little bit to make sure you're doing okay." And, with that, he strode off again.

Iain watched him go. "Does he ever walk, or is he always in a race?"

"I have seen him casually walk," she admitted. "Just not very often."

Iain smiled, nodded, and said, "It's like a lot of things in this place. There's a time for everything."

"And your time, so far," she said, "has been to rest and to recover. Your time to move forward will happen soon enough."

He nodded. "This afternoon, I think. Shane said yesterday it was time to switch things up."

"See?" she said. "You may not want to eat quite so much, at least not before your workout. Because, if Shane says he'll switch it up, chances are he'll *really* switch it up."

"It'll hurt tomorrow, won't it?" He wrinkled up his face. "I can handle pain, but I don't really like it."

"Nobody likes pain," she said. "We can all handle a certain amount of it. But nobody wants to get to the point where we tolerate it so much that we don't even feel it. Because to feel pain is to feel alive. And to recover from that hurt is to recover from what we went through. That means, realizing that every step we take moving forward are the steps that we're doing for ourselves, to improve our lives and to improve our future, now that we know that we actually have one."

He shook his head. "Heavy words."

"Enlivening words," she corrected. "Now let's eat."

IAIN SPENT THE next few days thinking about her words. Robin had a unique take on life, and maybe he needed that too. His reason for coming here was to experience a whole new beginning, but he had been very disappointed at his start so far. Shane explained he was just checking to see what Iain could do and what he couldn't do, trying to see where his weaknesses were and finding out what needed to be done.

But it sounded like the same old song Iain had heard time and time again. He felt that this was as good as his legs would get. This was what he had; this was all he had, and he had better make the best of it. When he woke up in the morning three days after that prophetic conversation with Robin in the cafeteria, Iain had gotten dressed and was sitting here when a knock came at the door. He called out, "Come in."

Shane poked his head around the door and said, "This morning's session might be a bit rough. I just wanted to warn you to eat light."

Iain looked at him in surprise, then slowly nodded. "Nothing has been hard yet," he said.

"I know," Shane said with a big smile, "but now it's time to get down to work." And he disappeared.

Iain wasn't sure if he believed Shane or not. It seemed like just more talk. The trouble was, if this was all Iain had to live with, was it even worth doing more? He figured it would be something he had to ask Shane about. But maybe it was too early to judge. Maybe Shane didn't know. Maybe Shane was being an eternal optimist.

For himself, Iain could feel that sense of wanting to just give up. That sense that nothing mattered. That this was it. He might as well leave the rehab center, save everybody the time and effort, and get a job somewhere. He didn't have a clue how or what skills he possessed, but he was sure that nobody would take an amputee. Why would anybody take on someone who obviously has physical issues when they could get an able-bodied individual instead?

Although some companies were definitely helping out veterans more than others. He'd even heard about that group in New Mexico, helping vets get back into the employment field. He was pretty sure he'd met Badger a couple times, and he was the one heading this new group. Iain wondered if he should contact Badger and see if similar work was being done here in the Dallas area that Badger might know of for someone like Iain. Hell, Badger's group had advanced prosthetics. Maybe Iain could get something that would work for him too. Make him more employable.

Refusing to allow himself to be daunted by the thought, he opened up his laptop and quickly sent an email. It took a bit to find Badger's company online. *Titanium Corp.* Once Iain found it, he stared, amazed to see the group photo of the men of steel, standing with their arms around each other. Their prosthetics were obvious, but the bonds were just as evident. With that, he grabbed the contact email and quickly sent Badger a message.

Looking at the picture on the main page, he knew at least three of the other men too. Iain's heart ached as he realized how much he missed that camaraderie, that sense of belonging, that knowing that you weren't alone in this world. That's how he felt right now, kind of adrift.

Even though he had a lot of physical support here, they wouldn't be there for his tomorrows. They wouldn't be the people who helped him make the shift from this end of his rehab to the next stage in his life. He'd come here with such high hopes of a new beginning, a chance to get his right leg to do so much more than it was doing. His back, even though strong, obviously couldn't handle the long truck ride and had set him back by days if not weeks. He felt tired, and he didn't know why, but it was more at a soul level.

He chose the wheelchair and wheeled his way to the cafeteria. He wasn't even hungry, and now he was worried about Shane's words. He headed for the coffee first and, with a hot mug, wheeled himself onto the deck. He sat here quietly, all alone, trying to figure out what was wrong with his world. He sat out in the sun, pondering life, hating this slump, but realizing that, instead of looking for new hope, he needed to look in a new direction. A direction that had a future.

As he sat here nursing his coffee, Dennis arrived at his back. "Hey, not eating today?"

He looked up at him, smiled, and said, "Shane warned me it could be a bit rough. Told me to eat light."

Dennis's frown was instinctive. "Maybe light," he said, "but you can't go with nothing. If your blood sugar's low, exhaustion will take over in no time. You don't want Shane thinking that you're in such poor shape that you have to quit again."

"No, I don't really want that," he said, "but I don't even know what *eating light* means anymore."

"I got you," Dennis said. "Give me a minute." He disappeared.

Iain didn't even particularly care what he brought. It would be food, and, as long as he ate half of what he normally would, he should be okay. At least he hoped so. Shane had set off a chain of events that Iain had been trying to calm down since they had talked. And yet, all Iain seemed to be concerned about right now was worrying and fussing and looking at a million different options, but none of them seemed even appealing or possibly doable.

When Dennis returned a few minutes later with a beautiful-looking bratwurst, scrambled eggs, and a piece of whole-wheat toast, he said, "This is about half of what you normally eat, so get some of this down, and then we'll plan for a better lunch for you."

"I could be sick to my stomach by lunchtime," he murmured, but he didn't believe it. He'd yet to see anything to match his expectations coming here.

Dennis nodded, and his tone turned serious when he said, "I've seen it before. I've seen guys come in exhausted and starving. They take one look at the food, and their stomach muscles heave right away. I don't know what Shane has planned for you. Just know that it's for your own good."

Iain gave a startled laugh at that. "Is it really for my own good?"

"Sometimes the methodology seems a bit rough or confusing," Dennis said. He placed both palms on the table and leaned forward to look at Iain. "But Shane is one of the best. If he sees something he can do to help you improve, then listen to him. He'll get you there."

"And I'm wondering if there's anywhere to get to," Iain said. "I've had no progress since I arrived. The last surgeon said this is as good as the right leg will get. Maybe I'm wasting everybody's time by being here. I should just go to town, rent a place, and find a way to do something with my days and to learn to live with my life as it is."

"Screw that," Dennis said. "That's a defeatist attitude. You just got here. I already heard that you were having a couple tough weeks because of your trip here. And now that you're here, don't give up. See what Shane has got to say first."

"Well, it sounds like you're in my corner," he said with a half smile.

"I'm in everybody's corner," Dennis said, "but especially the underdog. I want every one of you to get up and walk out of here to live happy, cheerful lives," he said emphatically. "And I've seen enough here to know what can happen. I know you're probably thinking that you'll be the one case that it doesn't happen to. I swear to God, I've seen time and time again the same attitude, the same thought process for almost every person who came through those front doors.

"You're also a big man, and you know that that leg won't handle you too much longer, no matter what the surgeons have done. You'll have to strengthen it. And Shane is the one to help make it stronger. Shane'll make it work and will support you. And he'll make sure that that back of yours is capable of handling everything that's still to come. You're young, and you could have some fifty more years," he said. "You want a body that can cradle you, can support you, and can work with you," he said. "So, whatever Shane says, you do it." He smacked the table and turned and walked away.

Realizing he'd been told off in a subtle way and not really understanding how or why, Iain dug into his eggs and bratwurst and smiled. They were, as always, very tasty. His stomach was happy to get some food. He stopped with that, finished off his coffee, then slowly made his way back to his room. There, he changed into his shorts and a muscle shirt and headed to his meeting with Shane.

As he wheeled into the room, Shane looked at the wheelchair in approval. "Glad you brought that today," he said. "You'll be grateful for it when we're done."

"You'll hurt me that much?" he joked. Iain wasn't exactly sure what today was supposed to bring. Of course, with everybody warning him, he could feel his own defenses and maybe a little bit of fear rising up. Like he had said to Robin, nobody liked to be in pain.

"It's not what I'll do to you," Shane said. "It's what you'll do to you."

He frowned at him.

Shane gave him a quick grin. "I promise I haven't killed anybody yet."

"And there's always the first," Iain announced. He rolled closer, parked the wheelchair against the wall, and said, "What are we doing?"

"Floorwork," he said. "I want to see what kind of stretching we can get out of that leg."

Still seated, he lifted his right leg and said, "How will we start?"

Shane looked at him in surprise, then shook his head and said, "No, we'll start with the leg missing the foot."

"And why would you want to start there?" he asked in surprise.

"Because it's been pulling more of its own weight than you'd expect and because the other one is so badly injured. The surgeries have helped, but you have a long road of recovery to get that right leg to pull its own weight. In the meantime, the left leg is the one hurting."

Iain stared at Shane in surprise.

Shane smiled and said, "Trust me. Let's start on that one, and then we'll get to the one that's just recovering post-op." And that's what they did.

Iain didn't think he could stretch, considering he only had 75 percent of that leg. He had the knee joint, but then the stump was about four inches down, and that was it. He'd hoped that having a stump would allow him to get a prosthetic, but, so far, that hadn't happened. And all because they were waiting to see what the right leg would do. It had to support all his weight. If only he wasn't such a big guy …

"Okay, let's get started," Shane said, and he put him through the paces. It seemed minor until twenty minutes later, when Shane took the exercises to another level.

By that time, Iain felt sweat flowing freely off his body. He gasped when he finally reached a break in his exercises and asked, "So, are we done for the day?"

Shane looked at him in surprise and said, "We won't be done until noon. Unless, of course, your body needs to shut down for a while?" Shane lifted an eyebrow, as if assessing Iain's condition and his willingness to do what was needed.

"Will this help me?" Iain asked. He was stretched out on the ground, supporting his weight on his elbows, as they had been working on the abductor muscles on the outside of his thigh.

Shane smiled, nodded, and said, "You don't understand the intricacies of what we're doing, but it's very important that you get your balance tuned up. With your balance back, you can regain your strength. Then we can get you walking normally on a prosthetic."

"I would love to get a prosthetic." But he hesitantly added, "They kept saying it would depend on my good leg."

"Honestly, your *good* leg is the one that'll get the prosthetic," Shane reassured him. "The bad leg is the one that we have to build up from surgery, and that's where we'll start now."

Iain frowned at him in shock. He stared down at his right leg and winced. "I don't think I'll like the next hour."

"I'm sorry," Shane said, "but I can guarantee that you won't like it one bit."

Chapter 6

ROBIN HADN'T SEEN Iain for a couple days. She went out of her way to check his room, but, so far, the door had always been closed. She changed up her breakfast and lunchtime hours, hoping to catch sight of him, but still nothing. Finally, on Friday morning, she asked Dennis if he'd seen him.

Dennis gave a solemn nod. "Shane started putting him through the heavy paces on Wednesday," he said. "He's not in very good shape."

Her eyebrows shot up. "Well, I guess that's good," she said slowly.

He looked at her tray and said, "What do you want for breakfast?"

"Yogurt and fruit," she said with a smile. "Maybe a little extra yogurt on the side."

"Or I could make you a parfait," he said in a teasing voice.

She smiled and nodded. "And I'm not saying no to that. You do make the best." And right in front of her, he layered fresh fruit, granola, cream, and plain yogurt until she had a beautiful concoction set before her. He handed it to her, and she carried it over to the coffee station. She poured herself a cup and stepped out into the sunshine.

She couldn't stop thinking about how Iain was surviving. He'd been afraid that what he had was what he would be stuck with, that his hope of a new beginning was useless, and that it wouldn't happen. Did he still feel that way? She glanced around, sitting in such a way that she could watch everybody come and go. But still saw no sign of him. She finished her breakfast, refilled her coffee, and headed to work. She and Stan had no shortage of appointments today, and she was kept busy right up to lunch. She was almost ready to miss lunch when Stan stopped in, looked at her, and said, "I don't even have the energy to go upstairs and grab food. How are you doing?"

"Same," she said.

He nodded, looked over at their receptionist at the front desk, and asked, "Annette, how are you doing?"

She looked at him, smiled, and said, "Why don't I run get food for both of you? What do you want?"

"What's on tap today?" Stan countered.

She picked up the phone and quickly called upstairs. Robin had to admit it was a huge boon to have food right now, right there, hot and ready.

"Something Spanish," she said with a shrug.

"That's fine," Stan said. "Get us two of everything."

Annette laughed. "How about I see what I can get on one tray."

"Or take the trolley," Robin suggested.

Annette looked at her in surprise, then nodded. "You know what? That'd probably be the best idea. Maybe I'll grab myself something too." The trolley was a teacart made out of stainless steel. She moved it to the elevator and disappeared from sight.

Stan and Robin looked around the front room, which was empty for once.

Robin said, "I feel like I shouldn't dare mention the fact that we're caught up because we'll immediately have a dozen vehicles pulling in the parking lot."

He laughed. "Isn't that the truth. And it's not even a surgery day."

"Thank heavens," she said. "Of course it's way worse when we're booked like this, and then we have emergencies coming in as well." She noted how tired Stan looked. "Are you sleeping okay?"

"Not last night," he said. "Don't know what was wrong, but I was walking around outside at midnight."

"I have done that a time or two," she admitted.

"How are you and Iain getting along?"

Her eyebrows shot up.

He shrugged and said, "I've seen you spending a fair bit of time with him."

"Not this week," she said with a shrug. "Apparently Shane started putting him through the paces, and Iain's been noticeably absent for the last half of the week."

"Well, it is Friday," he said. "If you wanted to spend some time with him this weekend, I'm sure that could happen."

"If he's in any shape," she said with a nod. "Maybe even just to get out to the pasture and lie down and sunbathe would be nice."

"Says you," he said. "I'll sleep. Besides, we'll have patients all weekend, so I'll be back and forth checking in on them."

"Right, we've got what? One dog and one cat for the weekend?"

"And then the regulars," he said. "That's why we have got to solve the Hoppers problem."

"Iain did say that he was pretty handy with a hammer and nails."

"If he were a little bit further down his healing road," Stan said, "I'd probably get him to come take a look, offer some suggestions on what we could do. What does Hoppers actually need?"

"Basically a covered outdoor run and a way to get back inside," she said. She walked over to the nearest window and studied the many dog runs they had. "Why can't we convert one of these to accommodate him?"

"There's an idea," he said, standing next to her. "Even if we just made him a smaller one off to the side."

They stepped outside and walked around to where dog runs were. They weren't huge, but they were large enough that dogs could stretch their legs, run back and forth, and somebody could throw a ball for them.

As they stood at the fourth one, she nodded and said, "We could even put a little doorway through here and make him a separate run." She studied the exterior of the building and then sighed. "But that'll mean giving him access through this big foundation wall."

Stan stepped to the side and said, "Well, what about using this nearby door instead? We could inset a bunny door in this side door and put another little small fence around here, cutting into the dog run, but redirecting to the side piece here, and then Hoppers can come and go as he wants to."

The two of them discussed it until they heard a shout from inside. They headed back in to see Annette pushing the trolley, fully laden. "Oh, that looks so good," Robin said. She looked around and said, "Why don't we just eat out here in the sitting room?" They sat around a small coffee table, with Annette joining them for their lunch break, and ate large plates of wraps filled with rice with raisins and curry spices.

"I don't know what this is," Robin mumbled with her mouth full, "but it's divine."

"I didn't even ask," Annette said. "I was so busy trying to get some of everything for you guys that I wasn't too bothered about getting the names of the dishes."

"If I care enough," Robin said, "I can always ask Dennis myself."

"True," Annette said with a smile. Only as they were almost done did Annette add, "And, by the way, I saw Iain up there."

Robin froze, looked over at Annette, and asked, "Really? Do you know who he is?"

She nodded. "I figured you two were friends. He was up there, and I just happened to notice," she said with a casual shrug.

Robin sat back, wondering if both Stan and Annette saw their friendship as something more. She frowned.

"Don't bother arguing," Stan said. "We can see the sparks."

"Not a whole lot anybody can do about sparks in his condition or mine," she said with a laugh. "And hardly *sparks*. More like, gentle interest."

"This is a place for friendships," Annette said quietly. "It's a place where any connection that's built here isn't built on the physical looks but built on gaining new strength, as people go from strength to strength."

"That's very insightful," Robin said. She laid down her fork, sat back, and rubbed her tummy. "That was great."

"It really was," Stan said, as he worked on finishing the

last bit on his plate.

Robin contemplated Annette's words because she was right. This wasn't a place where physical attraction was first and foremost. It was all about seeing the soul and the character residing inside the pain and also seeing the growth of the survivor in the patient's eyes. Not the physical body but the mental body, the emotional body, and how well people dealt with life. "I think Iain will have a few tough weeks," she said to Annette.

"He looked pretty wiped out right now," she said, "but he was glancing around, as if searching for somebody." And she let her words hang in the air.

Robin frowned.

"You may want to take the dishes up yourself," Annette said. "Not that I guarantee he'll still be there by now."

"Not likely," she said. "It's Friday. I don't know what his afternoon schedule looks like."

Annette nodded. "Probably like ours, which will be hellish." She pointed to the parking lot where three vehicles were pulling in at the same time.

Stan groaned, put the last bite in his mouth, snagged his coffee, and said, "I'll be in my office."

Robin laughed and said, "My coffee is gone. I'll return the dishes and grab another cup while I'm there." And, without giving Annette a chance to say anything and ignoring her smug smile, Robin grabbed the trolley and pushed it out of the lobby and the reception area. The last thing they needed was for clients to come in with patients and see food everywhere. She quickly closed the elevator door and zipped up to the cafeteria level. There, she pushed the trolley and headed toward Dennis.

Dennis smiled, took one look at the trolley, and said, "That's what I like to see. Empty plates."

"It was fabulous," she said. She quickly unloaded the trolley and grabbed more coffee. Then she caught sight of gooey melted chocolate chip cookies. She sighed and said, "I'll get fat here."

"I think that's a complaint everybody has," a man said behind her. She spun and saw Iain standing on his crutches, looking like he could collapse. Instinctively her hands moved out to his in an offer of support.

"Oh my," she said. "You look like you're done for."

"That bad, huh?" He squeezed her fingers and gave her a crooked grin.

"I've got about five minutes, if you want to talk," she whispered.

He shook his head slowly. "Honestly I'm not done yet. I have some more work to do at the pool, and then I have appointments this afternoon."

From his tone of voice, she could tell they weren't appointments he looked forward to. "I'm sorry," she said. "I'm around most of the weekend though, if you want to visit."

"That would be great," he said with a smile.

She looked at the clock on the wall behind him and realized that she didn't have five minutes at all. "Look. I'm really behind downstairs," she said. "How about I check in with you over the weekend? Maybe we can sit and have coffee or something." A smile flashed on his face, and it looked genuine. Tired and worn out but genuine.

He nodded. "If my door is shut, don't wake me though," he said with a half grin. "I might sleep through to Monday."

"And, if you do," she said warmly, "then you needed to."

With that, she dashed off, barely avoiding spilling her coffee on the trolley as she headed downstairs. But, as she bolted in, ready to tackle the afternoon's worth of work, she had a smile on her face. A knowing grin on Annette's face as Robin blasted past told her that her friend had taken notice too.

GETTING TO THE pool was agonizing. Iain didn't know why the hell Shane had been hiding all this from him through the first three weeks, and yet maybe Shane had been right to take it easy on Iain those initial weeks so the swelling in his back and both his legs went down. But getting to the pool today had almost maxed his abilities. He'd changed to the wheel-chair because absolutely no way could he manage crutches.

Once downstairs, he pulled to the side of the pool, locked the wheelchair, reached out a hand for the railing that would lead to the steps into the water, and slowly stood on his weak leg. Reaching for the second bar, he hopped closer. And then, with one final push, he jumped into the water.

As soon as the cool waves caused by his exuberance closed over his head, he felt some of the stress sliding off his shoulders. He didn't even want to surface. He wanted to stay under and float in a space where he didn't have to worry about his body not supporting him. A space where he didn't have to worry about his build being too much for his leg, where his oversized body—that he'd always taken so much pride in—was now going against him. A place where he could just relax and be free. But eventually he had to surface, and he did so slowly, releasing the air in his lungs and taking a deep breath of more. When he opened his eyes, Shane stood there with a frown on his face.

"That frown doesn't make me feel good," Iain muttered.

"You're done for the day," he said. "Here I was hoping

to get a few laps out of you, but you're too tired."

At that, Iain gave him a flat stare and said, "I can do at least two." And he started off with a front crawl. He still couldn't stop the rotation though, something that he knew would improve his strokes and would take away his exhaustion faster than anything because swimming was something he could get into a rhythm, and it didn't tire him.

He could go for miles, but, with only one whole leg, he found himself constantly rotating at the hip level. He focused on keeping his body straight and his legs moving from the thigh, not the foot. Realizing that that was where the mistake was, he slowed down his strokes and moved steadily forward. He came to the far wall, flipped, kicked off, then turned and headed back toward Shane. But he didn't stop there. He did another flip turn and headed back, finding it easier as his body loosened up a bit more.

After another eight laps, he came to a slowdown and stopped in front of Shane. "It's much easier if I remember to kick from the hip joint," Iain said.

Shane crouched in front of him. "I think that's one of the biggest lessons for anybody in this situation. You have to maintain your center of gravity and remember where your baseline is. Every set of joints is important all the way up, but you have to make sure that the spine and the hip joint are squared off to the rest of you and then stay that way."

"It's like relearning how to walk all over again," Iain said. "Now that I'm in the pool, I'm having to relearn how to swim."

"That's exactly what it is," he said. "I know it sounds funny, but, even if you just lost toes or half a foot, you would have a similar adjustment. It wouldn't be quite so large and exasperating, but you would still have to make an adjustment."

"Now what?" he asked. "I did ten laps. That's not a whole lot, but I am feeling a bit better."

"And you're looking a bit better," Shane said. "We'll do some stretches to finish off."

"Well, what stretches are to you," Iain said, "is a full-body workout to other people."

"And that's quite possible but hardly my concern though. I don't worry about other people. Let's worry about you."

"How do you separate the two?" he asked. He didn't know if he was delaying the stretches coming up—as the new muscles had to be gently teased into cooperating, when they didn't have any intention of doing so. It was like they tacked cement on or a steel bar from each muscle point to the insertion point.

"Partly it's my job," Shane said. "Partly it's experience. And partly I don't separate them. I draw from one experience to the other. The same as you need to draw from your old experience to now."

"I thought it'd be easier if I forgot all that beforehand."

"Sure," he said. "I want you to forget about the ten years in the navy before your accident, but I want you to remember way back to childhood, when you were still learning to do things. Where you had to learn to walk. Where you had to learn to bend over and touch your toes, and when you couldn't do it. All because the back of your legs weren't limber enough and your back didn't bend enough. And how it felt to actually stretch out all those muscles and get there."

"The thought of touching my toes ..." He shook his head. "That seems a long way away."

"It's not," Shane said. "Let's get started."

Chapter 7

W HEN ROBIN WOKE up Saturday morning, she laid in bed, tired and worn out. She'd been up to help Stan in the night, the two of them unavoidably coming in to check on a patient they were each worried about, only to find that both the dog and the cat weren't doing well. They'd stayed for a couple hours, until they were sure that their patients were improving. And then, they both crashed again.

Now she was lying in her bed on a Saturday, staring out and groaning. Stan would work a half day but another vet tech, one who came in to help when they got too busy, was here so that Robin had the full weekend off. But having the full weekend off when you lived beside the vet clinic didn't really mean you were *off*-off.

She often went in and checked on the animals kept there. Hoppers always needed to come outside; the horses and the llama needed grain and to be fed. And, even though that wasn't her job, she couldn't help feeling like maybe she should check outside to make sure it was being done.

As she sat up in bed and swung her legs to the floor, she groaned again. "If this is how I feel after a bad night, I can't imagine how Iain or the others feel." She stepped into a hot shower and realized that was a big problem, almost an impasse between them.

It's not that she couldn't understand, but it was outside her experience to fully comprehend. And she had to let him have the full experience of what he was going through and also honor that, without criticizing or in any way making it look like she could understand—because how could she? She could empathize and be grateful that she wasn't experiencing what he was, but absolutely she had no way to contemplate his situation to the same level which he was going through, day after day after day.

She'd been physically healthy all her life. She had worked with animals in difficulties and with major problems, but she couldn't do a whole lot to help any animal or any person without being an empathetic person. Yet that wasn't the same thing as being somebody who could say that she fully understood, had her own experience going through something the same, and could truly sympathize. Sympathy was fine and good, yes, in some situations, but that was the last thing she wanted to give Iain.

As she checked her watch after her shower, she realized she'd already missed the breakfast hour. But then that was okay because the last thing she wanted was food. What she really wanted was to go for a long walk out in the sunshine. She quickly braided her hair into a plait down her back, put on shorts, a decent walking shoe, and a T-shirt. Then she grabbed her phone and headed out to the animals. She had a bottle of water with her, and she'd do coffee and food when she got back.

She started off at the pasture with the animals, giving greetings and handfuls of grain to the horses and to the lovely llama that had joined them. Even the little filly was doing so much better, and she was definitely not the little-filly size that she had been before. She was growing every day. Her temperament was beautiful too, and she had an absolutely lovely blond mane.

Robin stood a moment, brushing the animals gently, just enjoying being with them. Finally saying goodbye, she headed off down the pasture where several acres of open land were. It could be more than that; she had no idea what an acre looked like down on the ground, and she wasn't sure what property belonged to the Hathaway House. She knew Dani did a lot of riding, in the mornings especially, and seemed to stay on the property and yet kept going for hours, so Robin didn't exactly know what property lines there were.

This morning she was just looking for something like an hour's walk. As she walked along the pastures and came up on the far side of a fence and walked all the way around, back to where she had started, she realized that that had already taken her the better part of an hour. She came up to the front parking lot and then walked to the veterinarian parking lot and went back to her own apartment.

Stepping inside, she thought about putting on coffee and then decided that maybe she'd go to the cafeteria and grab one instead. Inside, she was hoping that maybe her path would cross with Iain. Something was so very wonderful about him. She'd met a lot of the other men here, but they didn't have the same effect on her that Iain did. Maybe that was good. He was definitely the most interesting male she'd met in a long time.

As she walked inside, the cafeteria was empty, and all the trays clean and shiny, waiting for the lunch rush. She walked over to the coffee service, poured herself a cup, plus snagged a bottle of juice, then headed out to the deck. As she sat down, a voice hailed her. She turned to see Shane. She gave him a smile. "How are you doing?"

"I'm doing great," he said. "How are you settling in? It's been a couple months now, hasn't it?"

"Almost, yeah," she said. "And you?"

"Years and years and years," he said with a big laugh.

"Well, it seems like you're getting the job done," she said.

"How do you figure?" he asked with a questioning look in his eye.

"This place is such a success, and you are a huge part of that." She smiled. "A certain comfort is in that though," she said. She lifted her cup, blew at the hot brew, and added, "Not the least of which is you've had so many years of Dennis's cooking."

"I have, indeed," Shane said, patting his belly. "And eight years of trying to combat the extra waistline."

She burst out laughing. "I think that's a common complaint here."

He grinned. "So, how are you and Iain doing?"

She slowly lowered her cup and leaned forward. "Does everybody think something's going on between us?"

"Well, I personally notice things like that," he said. "And I know that Iain is often searching anytime he's out in the public spaces, as if looking to catch sight of someone."

"Might not be me," she warned.

"Might not be," Shane said cheerfully, "but I bet it is."

She could feel some heat flush her cheeks. She shrugged self-consciously and said, "Well, I must admit I hope he's looking for me," she said. "He's an interesting man."

"He is. He is also struggling in some ways."

"Why is that?"

"I don't think he thought it would be as hard as it is."

"I think he figured he had done as much improvement

as he could," she said. "This was kind of a last-ditch effort to go beyond what the surgeons had said. And then, when nothing happened in the first two to three weeks here, it's like he gave up. He was getting ready to walk away, giving up his bed for someone else who really needed it. With that thought, he had to start thinking about having a different life."

"I heard something like that from him," Shane said. "Only it's not that cut-and-dry. And he's a long way away from seeing his optimum self yet. And that's good."

"I'm glad to hear that," she said seriously. "We do a lot of very deep talking," she said with a half smile. "It's interesting getting to know who he is on the inside."

"It's one of the reasons I love my job," Shane said, "because the real person only shows up when trouble moves into their lives."

She thought about that for a long moment, then sat back and realized he was right. "You must have seen some incredible people throughout your years here."

"I have, indeed," he said. "It's been a joy and an honor to help these people."

"Do you have any concerns about Iain?"

He shook his head. "Not really," he said. "I think, as long as he's striving and still driving for something better than what he has, he'll be fine. We'll end up in trouble only if he gives up."

She frowned at that. "And is there any reason he would give up?"

"He'll come to a point in time where his body can't be improved anymore," Shane said. "When the muscles are as strong as they'll get, without expending more time and effort into building them up. Meaning, more energy than he has available."

She had to work her way through that convoluted explanation and then understood. "So, really there's a point where he'll max out his potential. Even here."

"Yes. To know if he's happy with where he's at then is hard to say."

"I know he really wants to get a prosthetic on that leg so the one that had all the surgery is strong enough to support him."

"And that may or may not come to pass," Shane said. "I know he'll try it no matter what we say, but that doesn't mean he'll like the end result."

"Right," she said. "And I guess that makes sense, even though it's sad to hear."

"It doesn't have to be sad," he said. "The thing to remember is that life is all about finding where you're at and going forward with what you have. There's a certain comfort in having hard rules to follow."

"If you say so," she said. "It seems very odd though."

"No," he said. "It's a good thing."

"Maybe." But she seemed doubtful at first. "I know what he really wants is to walk on his own two feet."

"We'll do our best to get him there," Shane said. "But it's not just about building up. It's also about letting go. It's releasing the stiffness from the muscles as well as the stiffness from his needs and wants. As much as this is a physical process, it's a mental one as well. That can be the hardest part." And, with that, he got up and walked away.

She sat here for a long moment, thinking about their conversation. She had never really considered that psychological part of the equation, but it matched up to what she could see in other people around her. Even with her brother

Keith. Only she hadn't really put two and two together. Because she dealt with animals, she didn't have to explain what was going on to the animal itself. She couldn't ask the animal to stretch and to do what it needed to do. They almost instinctively did it anyway.

She had seen some horrific injuries where, when she saw the animal next, they were completely comfortable with that. And, in some cases, they'd healed better than before. The human body was just as marvelous, but the human mind had the ability to stop or to start the healing process. She wondered if Iain understood that too.

When another voice called to her from the doorway, she shifted to see Iain standing there on crutches, a surprised look on his face.

She got up and walked her empty coffee cup to the sideboard for dirty dishes, then headed toward Iain. "Hey," she said. "How are you doing? I expected you to sleep all weekend."

"No," he said. "Not something I was intentionally trying to do. I felt like it, but I haven't even eaten yet." He glanced at Dennis, who was wandering around in the back. "But it looks like we still have an hour until lunch."

She nodded. "Do you need food though? Because I'm sure Dennis can get you something."

Iain laughed. "No, that's fine," he said. "I was just stretching out by walking up and down the hallway a bit. My shoulders are still pretty stiff."

"You can go for a swim in the pool," she suggested.

He studied her in surprise, then said, "Join me?"

She frowned, then nodded. "Sure. Why not?" she said. "It's a beautiful day out, and we still have at least an hour until we can eat."

"Did you not eat?"

She smiled, shook her head, and said, "No, I didn't. I went for a walk instead."

"Good," he said. "I'll meet you down at the pool in ten?"

She nodded and said, "Ten it is."

And they split at the doorway. She headed back to her apartment and quickly changed. She grabbed a cover-up and then a big towel and headed up to the pool deck. Self-conscious but grateful she was here first, she tossed off her towel and her cover-up, and dove in with a nice, clean breaking motion into the water. And as soon as she broke the surface, she kicked out strongly and did several laps.

When she slowed down, she noted somebody in the pool stroked out strongly beside her. She smiled and made one more lap with him, then waited at the pool steps for him. And finally Iain stopped his laps, looked at her, and said, "You're right. This was a good idea."

"It's a great way to loosen up muscles," she said. "And I find it helps me to loosen up my thoughts."

That startled a laugh out of him. "Interesting way to look at life again," he said. "I really like that about you."

She smiled and said, "I like that about you too."

IAIN HADN'T REALLY expected her to come to the pool with him, yet having her here beside him felt natural. Water was his element, where he didn't need both legs to stand; and he was as much a fish as any good swimmer was, so he could hold his own. He dove into the water, then came up several times, just loving the feeling of being free. "My muscles do feel a lot better."

"Good," she said. "I'll do a few more laps, so I can work up a bit of an appetite."

"I highly doubt that's an issue," he said. "Especially if you haven't even eaten anything and already did a long walk."

"No, maybe not," she said, "but I don't get enough exercise as it is. Plus I find that I get fairly stressed in my job too, since I worry about all the animals that come through the clinic. So this is a great way to unwind."

"Well, it's not that I need to unwind," he said, "but I do need to stretch."

"How are you finding Shane to work with?"

Iain looked surprised at her question, then glanced around to see if anybody was close enough to hear them. "I think he knows his stuff," he said. "I'm not sure I always understand his instructions though."

"I hear you on that," she said, "particularly if it's cryptic."

"It's often cryptic with him. Some of the instructions are dead straight with their wording. *Lift your arm, lift this way, move this direction,*" he said with a laugh, "but a lot of it isn't clear from Shane. A lot of it is much harder to sort out."

"You can always ask him for added clarity."

"I could," he said. "But sometimes it's almost like the confusion or the lack of clarity is part of the challenge, and I'm supposed to figure it out myself. As if, by figuring it out, I'll gain an extra reward in there for having done so." He shook his head. "Listen to me," he said. "I'm daft."

At that, she burst out laughing. "I'll race you." Without giving him a chance to respond, she started toward the far side.

He immediately dove in after her, his right arm and his

left arm finding that same steady rhythm that he used to be so good at. And, by focusing on keeping his hips level and flat, he plowed right ahead of her. When she finally got to the far side, he was already there, waiting.

She laughed. "You might not be able to walk fast," she said, "but you swim like a dolphin."

"I do," he said. "It was one of the reasons I was absolutely ecstatic to find out a pool was here."

"Have you recommended this place to any of your friends yet?" She stroked out slowly, heading to the shallow end with the steps.

He looked at her in surprise and then slowly shook his head, following after her. "You know what? I haven't. But I should."

"If you think it's helping you, then you should," she said. She nodded to the far wall. "I'll do another lap." But this time, she laid on her back and just floated her way to the far end.

He floated gently beside her. "I didn't even think about it," he said. "I met a couple guys at the other hospital. They were kind of stuck, figured that this was their life."

"Kind of like you, huh?"

He looked at her in surprise, then nodded slowly. "Yeah, exactly like me. They had the same mind-set."

"Makes you wonder if you didn't have that mind-set because everybody around you also had that mind-set. And the same for them. If they don't know that there's another way to look at life and if they don't see any progress, then maybe they won't know to expect that either."

"Huh," he said. "I may have to say something to them."

"And a place like this always is interested in helping as many people as they can," she said. "I don't even know that they have any beds available as my own brother is on the waiting list, but if your friends need a place ... get them on too."

"Well, I definitely think a couple guys might benefit from being here," he said. "Jaden is one. Lance is another."

"Tell me about them?" They had reached the far wall to the pool again, and they both hung on, kicking with their feet to stay afloat.

"They were teammates in a mission that went bad. A roadside bomb hit them. Jaden got badly hurt, his right leg damaged, then burned, and their vehicle overturned and landed on his right shoulder. His thigh bone took a lot of shrapnel, so he has more steel pins in that leg than bones. So he's got a leg, but it's pretty useless," he said. He gave a clipped nod. "Shane might very well do something about that."

"It's possible. And what about Lance?"

"Lance got shrapnel damage too I believe, but most of his injuries are structural, more so than external. He took several hits, clipped a lip off one of the vertebrae, took off the top head of his hip bone, and his ribs are just a mess."

"But he's in a VA hospital?"

Iain nodded. "One of his ankles was smashed, and he can walk, but badly."

"Sounds like maybe Shane or somebody else here could do a lot for him as well."

"I haven't even told him how I'm doing," he said.

"And that, I think, is because you thought this new beginning, this stage of life, was what you would have to live with," she said. "So, you didn't see that you had anything to tell them."

"But I was wrong," he said slowly. "As much as I hate to

admit it, Shane's work and knowledge of his field is amazing—and, no, I'm not really seeing any change yet—but, if it
doesn't happen, it won't be from Shane's lack of effort. And
maybe that's why I'm holding back because I'm not seeing
the progress yet."

"And how much are you holding yourself back?"

"What do you mean?" he asked, his forearms on the edge
of the pool to hold him up, his tone sharp. "I'd never do
something like that."

Chapter 8

HEARING THE HARSHNESS in his tone, Robin realized she was on delicate ground. "Sometimes I think that we don't always know how much we're holding ourselves back," she said slowly, swimming toward the pool ladder in the shallow end with the steps. He splashed beside her. He was willing to be mollified, but, at the same time, she could sense that he didn't really want to broach this. "Remember some of the heavy conversations we've had?"

"Sure," he said. "Sometimes they stick in my brain and just won't get out."

"Right. So, if your body is unyielding, maybe look for a place in your mind where your mind is unyielding."

His eyebrows shot up.

She shrugged. "I know I've had to do the same for myself," she said. "At one point in time, I wanted to be a vet. But I didn't want to be a vet just to be a vet. I wanted to be a vet because I felt that other people would then respect me more."

"How does that have anything to do with it?"

"Because I'd *be* someone," she said quietly. "But I had to realize that I had to be somebody inside before I could be somebody outside, at least according to somebody else."

He blinked. And then he nodded slowly. "I see what you're trying to say," he said, "but that's hardly my case."

"No, and it doesn't really seem to fit what I was trying to say either," she said. "I guess it's more a case of understanding who we are inside and realizing that what we believe about ourselves and what we believe about our progress and our own mental state affects who and what we are on the outside."

"I've said that a time or two myself," he agreed, his good mood apparently restored.

Yet somewhere along the line he hadn't got the message. She didn't really want to try again because it was just nice and friendly to be on the same page, but she could sense that something inside needed to be pried out for him to take a closer look at. "Well, I'm sure Shane has a lot to say about it too."

Iain nodded. "But, like I said, sometimes his instructions are a little convoluted."

"You mean, a little obscure?" she said with a bright smile. "Like you have to dig deep to understand what he's saying?"

Again, that sharp look came her way, and he nodded. "Something like that, yeah." He took a deep breath and said, "I think I'll get changed and then grab some food. I'm quite tired again."

"I'm sorry," she said immediately. "Was this swimming too much?"

"I don't think so," he said. "I think it was an accumulation of things over the long week."

As she watched from the pool, he made his way awkwardly to the wheelchair before he sat down with relief. "Do you want to meet at lunch?" she asked. When he hesitated, she felt her heart wrench slightly. And then she backed up immediately and said, "Actually, no, I might have a nap myself."

"Good idea," he said a little jovially, almost too happily. "I'll have a shower, and then I'll see. We have a two-hour window for eating."

"Have a good rest," she called out. And she made her way slowly to the steps in the shallow end, as she watched him leave. Leaving the pool with a heavy sigh, she grabbed her towel and sat down in the sun, despondent all of a sudden.

She shouldn't have brought it up. It was for Shane to do. Or the psychologist. Or another specialist she didn't know about. But she definitely felt a sense of Iain being locked on the inside, whether he knew it or not. And that lock had to open up and free him ever-so-slightly in order for him to see the progress that he sought.

Groaning, she realized she wasn't likely to see very much of him at all this weekend now. Somehow she'd just changed everything between them. And not in a good way. She grabbed her towel and quickly dried her hair, then wiped down her body and headed back to her apartment. She didn't even want to go in for lunch now.

Instead, she considered getting *away*-away, taking a drive into town, picking up a few things that she needed, maybe having lunch at a restaurant in town too. Just taking a complete break from here. A change of location was supposed to be good for the health of the body and the mind. And it would stop her from looking around every corner to see if Iain was there. Now that he hadn't even mentioned lunch, she knew that was a dead deal too.

At her place, she quickly dressed into casual clothing to head into town, then grabbed her purse and hopped into her vehicle and took the long drive out of the property. She needed a real break. Especially today.

INSTEAD OF GETTING dressed and heading down for food, he collapsed onto his bed, a little more worn out than he expected. Not from being physically tired. His mood was the flattest of all. Her words had struck a chord, as if she knew something he didn't, as if she'd heard something he hadn't, and as if she was trying to get him to see something he needed to see that other people saw, but he couldn't.

And, if one thing was guaranteed to piss him off, others talking behind his back would do it.

Or to think that other people knew something that he should know, but they were leaving it for him to figure out. One of his old girlfriends had been like that. His buddies had all known that she was having an affair, and they'd waited for him to figure it out. Nobody, not one of them, had nudged him in that direction to say, *Hey, take a closer look at what's going on here.*

He'd been so angry at the end of that relationship that he'd lost his friends at the same time. No, he hadn't really lost them. He'd walked away from them and realized they weren't exactly what he wanted in a friend. He knew it was the bro thing to do with some guys. To either tell all or tell nothing. And all of his bros—apparently—had been of the *tell nothing* variety. This just brought all that back up again too. And it sucked. Who needed that crap?

Now that he was collapsed on his bed, he had a two-hour window before he needed to get food. Otherwise he would have to wait again. And he hadn't had breakfast either. He closed his eyes, willing his body to relax and to drop off for a short nap. Yet, every time he closed his eyes, he saw Robin.

He should text her and see if she was willing to meet him for lunch after all. Or not. Maybe it would be better to figure out her words first. Sometimes one had to go it alone, and just no other way would make it happen. And then he remembered Bruce and how long it had been since he'd contacted Iain. Or Iain had contacted him. So Iain quickly grabbed his phone and sent his buddy a text, checking in to see how he was.

Bruce answered almost right away. **Hey, we extended our stay once again, so we just got back two days ago. How are you?**

Good, Iain typed with a smile as he responded. **Working hard. How was your trip? Successful?**

That's great. And yeah we're giving us a second chance. Had like another honeymoon after we talked things out. And you? Making progress?

That was great news on Bruce's relationship. Yet Bruce had asked that same question that Iain hated so much, and he didn't even know what to say. He tossed down his phone, punched his pillow, and closed his eyes. He willed sleep to take him under so he didn't have to answer. And, when his cell buzzed again, he bet it would be Bruce again. Iain ignored it. At least for the moment, he needed to just be alone and to figure this out for himself.

Chapter 9

ROBIN KEPT GLANCING at the purchases she'd made a couple days ago. She was getting ready for work, but her gaze kept falling on the bag with the two journals in it. She didn't know why, but something about them had caught her eye. She's been in the dollar store, amazed that items of such quality were at such a cheap price. It had been almost like fate calling to her. She wanted something like this for herself to work through some of her own issues, realizing that it had been a long time since she'd had a relationship. Also noting that she was still, although she didn't mean to, looking at every man and judging him. Until Iain.

After meeting him, talking to him, she found that things in her life had focused in on this time, on this person, and she realized that she needed to be the best that she could be too. And that was likely way too New Age–sounding for anyone. She groaned and finished brushing her hair, braiding it up nicely and then walked over to pull both journals out of the bag. They were nice and simple, almost masculine looking, but had enough of a feminine touch to make her smile. She left one on the table and reached for the matching fountain pens that she had bought too.

"This is way too quirky," she muttered. "*His and hers,* when there isn't even a him and a her yet is a little bit pushy."

But she tucked the journal into her scrubs pocket, grabbed a fountain pen, and stuffed it into her other pocket. Then she headed into work. Sometimes, in life, one had to take a chance. She may have already pushed it too far with Iain that last time they were together in the pool, but she realized that was just part and parcel of this journey. If he wasn't for her, then fine. If she wasn't for him, well, maybe not so fine. But still, it's something that she would live with. At least she hoped she could.

She worked through her morning, kept busy with a steady stream of clients and animals, from clipping toenails to changing the tomcat's way, to stitching up another cat that had gotten into a scrap, and then a dog with a boil to be lanced. By the time she was done, she called out to Stan and said, "I'm heading to lunch."

"I'll leave here in another ten minutes or so," he said, distracted. "I've got a bunch of paperwork I need to finish up."

"That's because you're the boss," she said, laughing.

"Don't remind me," he groaned.

Still smiling, she headed upstairs to the cafeteria area. She had both the journal and the pen in her pockets still. And she was still of two minds as to whether she should give it to Iain or not. She didn't want to push him or to make him feel uncomfortable, and she was likely to do both.

In the cafeteria, she took a long look around. So many people were here that it was hard to see if Iain was around or not. She walked over, got into line, and, when she got up to Dennis, she asked him, "Have you seen Iain yet?"

He was busy serving people ahead of her, but he glanced back, frowned, then shook his head. "You know what? I don't think I have." She nodded and grabbed a large salad, but he shook his head and handed her a plate with a rack of ribs.

She nodded with joy. "I'll never say no to your ribs."

"You better not," he said. "You'll make me overhaul all my recipes again."

At that, she laughed joyously. "You have the best recipes."

"Me and Grandma," he said with a nod. "We're forever trying to outdo each other."

"Keep it up," somebody said behind her. "Because we're the ones getting the benefit of it."

Dennis's big grin flashed. "Yeah, that's why I do it."

Robin moved down and grabbed a cup of coffee and a glass of water and then sat outside in the shade. She'd been craving this heat, and now it was too hot for her. She sat in her corner up against the wall and ate quietly, loving the food, especially the ribs. When she was done, she sat back and sipped her water, looking at her cold coffee. "I should remember to not get the coffee at the same time," she muttered.

Dennis had been working his way through the tables, cleaning up dishes, when he heard her and said, "I'll get you a fresh cup."

"You don't have to serve me," she said, pushing her chair back to stand up.

"But if I don't serve you," he said with a smile, "I'll be serving somebody else. And there's nothing wrong with serving you, so let me do this."

She frowned at him. "Don't you have help to clear all this?"

His grin widened. "But it's not about having help," he said. "I enjoy this. I enjoy having the time and the opportunity to talk to everybody. Collecting a few dishes won't hurt me. Not only that but it also keeps me humble." And, with that, he took off.

She sat back down, wondering, because he did have a great attitude to life, and they could all learn something about that from him. When he returned with a fresh cup of coffee, she murmured, "Thanks."

He looked at her quizzically. "Something on your mind?"

"Just contemplating the convoluted way that we look at life."

"Ah," he said. "Those kinds of questions."

"Do you ever get hung up on them?"

"I try not to," he said. "*Hung up* is not an easy way to live. You've got to keep things flowing. Otherwise you're stuck, and you can't move forward. And we're never stuck for the reason we think we are."

"I've heard that phrase used regarding anger," she said. "Like we're never angry for the reason we think we are, but I've never really understood that. I guess what you're really saying is, we have to dig deeper to find the true reasons for our actions."

He grinned and nodded. "Something like that." Then he took off again.

She sat here, wondering what her reasons were for buying the journals. She really just wanted to give Iain an outlet that, if he didn't want to talk to her, and he didn't want to talk to his psychologist, Iain could hopefully work out his own problems himself. And, with that, she stood, her coffee cup in her hand, and headed toward his room. When she knocked on the door, she got no answer. But the door itself didn't appear to be quite latched because it pushed open ever-so-slightly. She pushed it open a little bit wider and called out, "Iain, are you there?"

Still no answer. She poked her head around the door, but his bed was empty. She walked in, placed the journal and the pen on his bed, and then walked back out again. He wouldn't necessarily know it was from her, but she could always send him a message later. On that thought, she frowned, walked back over, picked up the pen, and on the first page wrote a simple note, saying, *This might help you work your way through things.* And walked out. She hated to admit it, but, as she left, her footsteps increased in speed so that she was almost running. No *almost* to it. She *was* running away.

WHEN HE GOT back from his session with Shane, he found a little leather-bound book and a pen on his bed. He looked at it as he slowly stripped off his hot and sweaty clothing. He wanted a shower and then to head out for some food. It had been a rough morning and an even rougher weekend. He couldn't help but feel like he was pushing Robin away, and that made no sense to him because he really wanted to be friends with her and potentially see if they had more than that between them.

Of all the women he'd met in his life, she was the only one who had shown any interest in who he was now. And that meant everything to him. To create a relationship in a place like this meant seeing each other with all the ugly bits and pieces showing. And also a lot could be said about a woman who could like who he was now. And maybe, if he was lucky, even fall in love with who he was right now.

It had to be a good thing because she'd be seeing him for who he truly was, instead of the image he may have projected before. And no doubt he was a very different person now than before. He'd still been a good man regardless, but he'd been cocky and sure of life, sure of what he was doing. At least he tried hard to project that image. Whereas now he'd had his feet knocked out from under him. Literally.

After his shower, he made his way back to his bed with his crutches, a towel wrapped around his hips and a second one in his hands to dry off his hair. He sat down on the side of the bed, groaning with the effort.

No doubt something was going on inside him because he could feel himself resisting Shane, resisting everything he was pushing Iain forward to.

Whether it was Iain's belief this was all a waste of time, he didn't know. He was dealing with so much pain, and he was at this point in time where it didn't seem like there was any progress, so why bother? And yet Shane was so encouraging and seemed so cheerful and happy about Iain's work that it's almost like a disconnect existed between Shane and Iain. Or at least between him and the reality of his body.

Iain didn't see any change, didn't see putting his body through all this for no change whatsoever, whereas Shane said he definitely saw an improvement. Iain couldn't see it, and he was so caught up in the pain and the torture that he was going through on a daily basis right now that it was hard to see anything optimistic. He wanted to believe Shane, but how was Iain supposed to do that?

He picked up the notebook, then opened the front cover and read the note. His eyebrows shot up. "Well, you definitely bought this for me," he murmured. He looked at the fountain pen and smiled at the old-fashioned tool. It brought back memories of school days where he'd taken a calligraphy course for an easy elective class, something that he'd really enjoyed at the time. But he wasn't much of a writer, so he hadn't really found a whole lot of purpose in it.

Putting the two gifts on his bed, he dressed slowly and grabbed his wheelchair, knowing that, in his mind, it was a cop-out, but everybody else would say, *You have to save your energy for another day.* Then he headed down for his lunch. As soon as he got into line, Dennis was there.

"Robin was looking for you earlier," Dennis said. "She has already gone back to work now though."

"I had a rough morning," Iain admitted. He looked at the food and sighed. "It all looks so good. But I don't have too much strength or energy to eat."

"You can always have one plate now, and, if you need more, you can come back," he said. "What can I get you?"

Today was Chinese day because he saw noodles and stir-fry and ribs maybe, but how did that work? Still, he went for the ribs and a big plate of stir-fry.

Dennis nodded with a big grin. "Now I approve of these choices," he said. "They might seem like they don't go together, but you've got something for the soul and something for the body here."

Iain looked at him in surprise. "I kind of like the way you separated those."

"Separated and yet joined together," Dennis said. He handed him the full plate. "You need a hand?"

"No," Iain said. "I'll be fine." And moving slower than normal, he headed his wheelchair over to the closest empty table. There, he put down his plate and dug in. He was halfway through the vegetables when he realized he'd left the ribs on the plate for later. His body did need the nutrition.

Dennis arrived soon afterward with a large glass of water and a glass of milk. "I don't think you're getting too much calcium these days," he said. "So you can get that down."

"Not a problem," he said. "I do like my milk. And I guess, if I'm not eating yogurt or cheese, milk is the easiest way to calcium, isn't it?"

"Any reason you don't like cheese or yogurt?"

"I like them both," he said. "I just don't tend to eat very much of them."

"You might want to think about changing that," he said. "I get that you're building muscle and nerves and trying to regain your strength, but your bones also have taken a huge beating."

"Well, I don't have a problem drinking milk," he said. He picked it up and had a big gulp. He really loved the taste as it slipped down his throat.

"We can add one to your meal every time now," Dennis said.

"That would be good," he said, and Dennis disappeared at that. Iain finished off his vegetables and tucked into his ribs. By the time he was done, he pushed his plate back ever-so-slightly and just relaxed. The drive had been to get here before the lunch hour closed, and, now that he'd accomplished that, he could feel the fatigue setting in. Particularly with a full belly.

He had appointments this afternoon—not with Shane, thank God—but with one of the doctors and maybe his psychologist? That would never be an appointment he looked forward to. But still, it was something he couldn't get out of. He slowly made his way back to his room, picked up the notebook, smiled, and realized he hadn't had a chance to say thank-you but tucked it into the pocket on the side of his wheelchair along with the pen. Then he grabbed his iPad and checked his schedule. With that on his lap, he headed toward the office where he was expected.

As he wheeled in, Dr. Broker looked up, smiled, and said, "How is Iain today?"

"Tired, sore, partially wondering why I'm still here," he said.

The doctor looked at him in surprise; then he glanced down at his paper file and flipped through a few pages and said, "Tell me about it."

Just like a dam had been broken, Iain explained how he'd come for this new beginning, and yet, when there was no progress and still wasn't any progress, he now realized that he needed to make peace with what he had and move on from there. So, it felt like he needed to cut short his time at Hathaway House.

"And yet everybody else seems to think you're making great progress," the doctor said, sitting back and playing with the pen in his hand.

Iain's eyes studied the pen as it twirled around and around.

"But *I'm* not seeing the progress," he said quietly.

"What are you seeing?"

"Somebody who needs to face the reality of his situation," he said. "Realize that this is it. I need to accept what I am and go on from here."

"And what are you?"

And this was just one of the reasons why Iain hated coming to these visits. The constant questions, the constant searching, the constant looking for answers and realizing that the answers he had were not necessarily the same answers everybody else had. "A disabled man who needs to find a way to lead a fulfilling life."

"Okay," the doctor said. "And what do you say about everybody else having seen progress?"

"All I see is pain," he said. "Every session with Shane hurts."

"He can ease it back," the doctor said quietly. "We don't want you in so much pain that it becomes a problem."

"It's not," he said, "but it does feel very much like I don't need to work that hard."

"So, if it's not hurting too bad, and you're still attending all his sessions, and he's seeing progress, what do you think the problem is? Or is it a case of you can't see what's right in front of you?"

Iain snorted at that. "That's quite possible," he said. "Do we ever?"

The doctor smiled. "Sometimes we don't see very clearly at all," he said. "It's interesting that I have such positive reports from everybody but you."

"I don't know about that," he said. "I did have somebody mention that maybe I had a bit of an inflexible attitude."

At that, the doctor's eyebrows rose, and the corner of his mouth twitched. "And do you think so?"

"I didn't think so," he said, "but maybe. Maybe I just had it locked in my head that the surgery would be the be-all and end-all and put me back on my feet. When I realized that it would only partially put me back on my feet and that both my legs were still weak and that I was still suffering, then I just locked down on that."

"What will you do to ease that?"

He just gave him a flat stare. "I have no idea."

The doctor nodded slowly. "Do you have a journal?"

He stared at him in surprise. "Somebody just gave me a notebook and a pen to do something along those lines."

"Maybe instead of judging yourself, just open up your mind and open up to a page and see what comes up? See how you feel about your whole situation. See if you really feel like this. See if this is a blockage or if this is something you're trying to avoid."

He frowned. "What could I possibly be trying to avoid by doing better?"

"Success," the doctor said bluntly. "So many people sabotage their own world in order to avoid becoming a success. Success is scary."

"Success would be to get my body back," Iain said harshly. "How is it I could possibly be afraid of that?"

The doctor looked him straight in the eye and said, "And that's what I want you to tell me when you come back here next week." With that, his phone rang on the desk. He picked it up and answered it.

Iain didn't even hear the conversation. He slowly wheeled himself back out and headed to his room. That was just another one of the reasons he hated these conversations. Nothing was ever clear; nothing was ever laid out. He was very much a person who, if he was told two plus two made four, then it made four.

But this kind of mental crap just seemed like an endless gamut of right and wrong answers, and it was a minefield. He didn't want to walk a minefield anymore; he wanted to know that what he was doing was right and correct and would lead exactly where he wanted it to. The trouble was, he no longer knew where that was.

Before he came here, he'd been all about making that last surgery a success. And when it hadn't been, he'd come here thinking that *this* would be the answer. But he quickly realized it wasn't the answer either. This is just who he was, where he was, and what he had to get used to. So, what the hell did the doctor mean?

Confused, irritated, and frustrated, Iain made his way to his room and realized that, with all the appointments he had had this afternoon, it was already four o'clock. He wanted desperately to have a swim, but he was edgy and didn't want to be around people.

By the time he made his way to the bed, he crashed and stared at the window. Was he afraid of success? Was being a failure more comfortable? What a horrible thought. What did being a failure mean? In a place like this, he got a lot of attention, he got a lot of help, he got a lot of assistance, and he got a lot of service from others. Was he such a poor human being that he was more concerned about receiving attention than doing things on his own?

He was used to being severely independent. What had happened to that? And was it success or really the fear of failure again? Because what if he was a success and then failed at that too? When he heard the words in his mind, he winced. He slowly picked up the journal, looked at it, groaned, then reached for the pen and started writing.

Chapter 10

SEVERAL DAYS LATER, when she kept looking out for Iain but never saw him, Robin realized just what an omega-size problem she had with him. A part of her felt lost without him here, without seeing him on a regular basis, without even just touching base and moving along that pathway of friendship and knowing that they were both together and caring about each other. No doubt she cared about him. She cared about his recovery. She cared about the life that he was leading, whether it was messed up right now or not.

By the following Friday, she was once again looking at her weekend and wondering if she should go into town and spend a day there as a break. At two o'clock in the afternoon after a particularly rough day, she'd come up to grab five minutes and a cup of coffee and a bite to eat. She had missed lunch. Dennis, when he'd seen her, had shaken his head and *tsk*ed, then had brought her a huge sandwich. It was lovely. Every vegetable she could possibly imagine being slapped between two slices of bread. Protein was in there too. She thought it was ham or maybe roast beef but also peppers and onions and lettuce and tomatoes and cucumbers and pickles, and it just went on. She smiled as she munched her way through it. It was a sandwich to make her soul smile.

When Dennis appeared a few minutes later, holding a pot of tea in his hand to deliver to a table beside her, she looked at the tea in surprise. "I never thought of having a pot of tea here."

He looked at her. "I've got lots of little pots," he said. "Any time you want a pot of tea here or to take to your office or back home, you just let me know."

"I hate to disturb you."

"Ah, ah, ah," he said. "None of that. We already went over that once. If you want something when I'm not here, the cupboard underneath the coffeepot has a few teapots just for that purpose."

She smiled, nodded, and said, "Fine, maybe I'll take a pot back with me."

"You do that," he said.

And just like that, he was gone again.

She wondered if she could do the job that he did and still have the same attitude. It was a job that offered so much pleasure to so many people, and yet much of the world looked down on it. They'd say he was just bussing tables or whatever derogatory term that people could slap on him at the time. And yet something was almost spiritual about what he did. She didn't even mean it in a necessarily religious way but didn't know how else to describe it.

It's as if he passed out joy and advice freely, and everybody felt better that they had seen him that day. Kind of like the way she felt when she saw Iain. The trouble was now, she hadn't seen him in days, not since she'd given him the journal. She had received no response from him, no acknowledgment, nothing. He hadn't sought her out nor had he found a way to thank her over the phone, if he even knew how to find her. But then he could have called the veterinarian clinic at any time.

Depressed, she finished off her sandwich, pushed her

chair back, and stood. She carried the dirty dishes to the waiting trolley and headed down the back stairs to see the horse called Appie and the llama named Lovely. Both of them raced over to visit. She scratched the big horse and the beautiful little llama, enjoying the chance to connect with them.

When she looked across the hill, she could see one of the men lying in the tall grass. He was beside Hoppers. *Hoppers was free?* She frowned as she watched, but the rabbit didn't appear to be bothered about going anywhere. A lot of fresh green grass surrounded him, and he was nibbling and nudging his way over each blade. Stan must have let Hoppers go outside with this man in order for Hoppers to be here, and that surprised her too. Stan didn't do that lightly. She wandered closer and then recognized Iain.

He looked at her, smiled, and said, "There you are."

She reached out a hand, palm up, and said, "I've been here all along."

"Nope," he said, an odd note to his tone. "I came down to find you, but you weren't there."

"Ah," she said. "I missed lunch, so I went to grab a bite of something to get through the afternoon."

"I bet Dennis didn't let you get away with that without making you something special, did he?"

She laughed. "Absolutely not. Our Dennis is so very special."

"He cares," Iain said simply. "I've come to understand that that's all it is. He cares. He comes from the heart."

She sat down beside him, watching as Hoppers meandered another few inches over. "Stan let you bring Hoppers out?"

"I think he asked me to bring him out specifically," Iain

said drily. "Apparently you're still looking for a pen for this guy."

"We'd love to leave him loose, but he's just as likely to end up on the road and get hit by a car than anything."

"He's pretty big for a predator to take on, which would be the normal danger we'd expect of a rabbit."

"Yep, but anything big enough that could take him down would get several good meals out of him," she admitted.

He just grinned, reached down, and gently rubbed Hoppers's back. Hoppers didn't seem to mind in the least. "I never had a rabbit as a pet," he said. "Never really considered it."

"And would you now?"

"I'm not so sure," he said. "But he's definitely peaceful to be around. Again, kind of like Dennis. They come from joy."

She loved that. "I hope you wrote that down in your journal."

"What, that Hoppers comes from joy?" he asked, laughing.

"I think that we should strive to come from joy," she said quietly. "If I end up learning that lesson before I die, I'll consider this life one well-lived."

"Hadn't thought about that," he said. He looked over at Lovely and Appie, the llama and the horse wandering toward them and said, "They all do though, don't they?"

"They do. They're full of forgiveness. They're full of joy. They're full of just being who they are," she said. "I have to admit, I'm jealous."

"Why? What part of you isn't good enough?" he asked with a sideways look.

"The insecure, scared-to-brave-the-whole-new-world me," she said. She hopped to her feet and dusted the dirt off her butt. "As much as I'd like to stay here and talk, I'm expected to work this afternoon."

"I took the afternoon off," he said. "I just thought maybe you'd meet me at the pool at say four o'clock or whenever you're done."

She hesitated, looked at him, looked at the pool, and then nodded. "It's a date." And she disappeared back inside.

IAIN WATCHED HER go, a smile playing on his lips. Hardly a date but, hey, he'd take what kind of a date facsimile this could be anyway. He should have thanked her for the journal but hadn't. He'd have to remember to do so when she came back out. He was feeling kind of odd and spacey himself.

Once he'd started writing in the journal, it seemed like he couldn't stop. Now he'd covered pages and pages. He didn't know if that was good or bad, but it was something that he seemed unable to change. Finally he got up, his thoughts heavy, and looked down at Hoppers. Iain was wondering what to do about the rabbit, when Stan called out to him. He looked over, and Stan walked toward him. "I'll bring him back to his hutch."

"It seems like such a shame," he said. "It's a perfect pasture for him."

"I know, but he's not exactly house-trained, and he won't stay close by without a fence of some kind. And we don't want to put him in with the horses either."

"Right. Gotta keep him safe," he said. He watched as Stan crouched and picked up Hoppers. Hoppers made absolutely no effort to get away and instead cuddled into Stan's neck. Iain grinned. "You're really blessed to be doing the work you do."

"I am," he said. "I think that's one of the joys of being in this world. We get to make choices. I'm happy to say I made a good choice." With that, he headed back inside.

And that left Iain wondering if everybody in this place was full of those heavy New Age comments. Because of all the choices he'd made, he'd been absolutely ecstatic with his. To go into the navy and making it into the SEALs had been his best day. But now? Now he had a whole pile of new choices. None of which he felt qualified for. Or none involved where his joy of being in this world was, like Stan talked about. And that brought Iain back around to the doctor's question about whether Iain was afraid of being a success.

Maybe the question really was if he was afraid of being a failure.

Slowly, his heart heavy, he made his way back to his room on his crutches, and, as soon as he sat on his bed, he reached for the journal and started writing again. And again, the words just flowed. Some of it didn't make any sense and didn't seem to matter as his hand flew across the page. He realized he would run out of pages before too many days had gone by. He made a concerted effort to write neater, smaller, only to give it up because it seemed to impinge on his ability to let the words flow. The deluge was everything from his childhood to the problems he'd had in the navy to waking up in the hospital. None of it was very important alone— barring the event leading to the hospital—but all of it mattered.

He shrugged. "That makes no sense."

But it did because individually they weren't big for the most part, but, when the memories were added in the mix, they became one much bigger issue. Because of what he was doing right now. He was trying to figure out just what he wanted to do with his life, something that he hadn't had to do ever because he had always wanted to join the navy. And now he was no longer in active service but had money to go back to school, if he wanted to, and the world was wide open to him. And yet Iain had no idea what to do. And he realized that really what was going on—maybe for the first time in his lifetime—was fear of making the wrong choice, which he was pretty darn sure was really his fear of being a failure again.

Somehow, in that crooked, twisted mind of his, he'd decided that the accident had been his fault, ending up where he was—which was also his fault—and not having a foot. His fault too. He shouldn't have taken that damn route. If he'd gone the other way, none of this would have happened.

He'd come here *not* planning to be a failure, but he hadn't planned to be a success either.

And somehow that seemed important. He searched Google for *planning to be a success* and *not planning to be a success* and found many videos and blogs on it. He picked up his laptop, sat down, and listened to some of the recordings. Several touched him and highlighted his situation.

So much of it was about goal setting. His goal had been to get here to Hathaway House and to leave that old persona behind. Which he had done. But then he'd been in a state of existing, adjusting to what this life was all about here. He'd thought he'd been adjusting to life as it was physically now and would carry on. And Shane had kind of blown that because, according to Shane, there had been a ton of progress.

If there was this ton of progress, then Iain had to adjust again and do what? He would have to adapt. He stared out the window of his room, wondering why adapting and seeing progress would hurt. And he was pretty sure it was because he was afraid. Afraid that he'd still be this person who had to adjust and to adapt to whatever he had.

Maybe the bar would be up that tiny little bit, but it wouldn't be enough to make a difference. He wouldn't ever be whole.

He took a slow deep breath as that realization hit him. Because, of course, he would *never* be whole again. He'd lost a part of himself. He'd lost part of his leg, and somehow losing a piece of his physical body had meant that he'd lost a whole chunk of his emotional body too. Part of his soul. And that was wrong. Because, although that physical piece was missing, there was no reason that the rest of his person couldn't go on as being deemed whole and happy. But somehow he got sucked into believing that, because he was missing a foot and part of his shin, all of him was missing something. He hadn't planned to be a success—which meant "whole" in his mind—and, therefore, he was a failure because he had failed to plan for being a success, even without his foot.

With his head shaking, he looked at the clock and realized it was four. He really didn't want to go down to the pool now though. His mind was too busy churning on everything rolling through it. But he also knew that he felt a sense of grounding when he was around Robin. A sense of calmness and peace surrounded her, and, right now, with this hurricane going on in his heart and his mind, he really needed those things.

Slowly and carefully, he got dressed in his loaned swim trunks, grabbed a towel, and then moved himself to the wheelchair and headed to the pool to meet up with her. He just hoped that they could avoid too many heavy conversations. His heart was already struggling. And it shouldn't be that way. When he got to the pool, he found her already there, sitting on the edge, leaning back on her hands, facing the sun. She was just resting, her eyes closed, enjoying being done with a hard day's work, facing the weekend, and ready to spend some time with him. And he realized that, once again, he hadn't been planning to succeed with her either. He'd just been putting in time, hoping that maybe something would happen. But he hadn't taken any concrete steps to actually see that it did happen.

He sighed and slipped quietly into the water, then swam toward her.

She didn't even open her eyes when she asked, "Hey, how you doing?"

"How did you know it was me?"

"I recognized the heavy sigh," she said with a bubbling laugh, opening her eyes.

He looked at her in surprise.

She smiled, nodded, and said, "You're going through some heavy-duty stuff these days. Heavy sighs are part of that."

"So, when I solve some of these big issues, do they stop?"

"I think so," she said, cocking her head to the side. "I actually think they do."

He grinned. "Are you ready to do some swimming, or are you're just going to sit there like a sunny mermaid?"

Chapter 11

"I NEED TO do some swimming," Robin said. "I get so little exercise these days." She slipped into the water beside him, and together they started doing laps. As a Friday after work went, this one was pretty peaceful. She'd had a long, hard day, but she was looking forward to the weekend. Iain appeared to be working his way through some stuff, and that was always good. She didn't want to push, and she certainly didn't want to open up the topic, but he appeared to be almost incapable of relaxing. "Maybe we should just lie in the sun and rest for a bit," she said.

He gave her a distracted look and then nodded. "That sounds good." They made their way up poolside, and she watched as he sat on the edge and grabbed his towel, then dried off his good leg and used the ladder to hop up. Then he used the railing to cross the few steps to one of the loungers.

"Would it help if I brought the wheelchair closer?"

He looked at it, then shrugged and said, "I can get it later."

She studied its location and said, "I'll move it, just in case." She unlocked the bottom of the wheels and brought it back over, then parked it beside him and crashed on the lounger beside him.

"Does it bother you?"

She tried hard to figure out what the question really meant because she wasn't sure what he was asking. She looked at him and said, "The wheelchair?"

"That I have a disability."

She smiled, loving the fact that he didn't say he was disabled. "We all have a disability," she said. "Sometimes it's physical, and everybody can see it, and sometimes it's internal, and nobody can see it. But none of us are perfect. We're all dealing with something."

He looked at her in surprise and laughed. "I hadn't seen it from that point of view," he said. "And lately it seems like all I do is think about some pretty heavy-duty issues."

"We all do," she said. "Or at least I do. There are definitely good things and bad things in life right now."

"Did you buy yourself a journal too? And thank you for that, by the way."

"You're welcome," she said with a pleased smile. "I was really surprised when I found them."

"I haven't used a fountain pen since I was in high school," he said.

"I never used one before," she said. "It's taking a bit to get used to."

"I'm enjoying it."

"I am too," she said, "but I tend to leave blotches."

He laughed at that. "Me too, but whatever."

"So it's helping?"

"I don't know if it's helping or not," he admitted, "but I'm certainly filling the pages."

"Good," she said. "Then it's helping."

"Maybe, the words sound like the ranting and raving of a crazy mind," he said with a laugh.

"It still helps to get it out," she said. She shifted under

the sun and closed her eyes. "I don't want to sleep out here because that sun will turn me to a fried crisp very quickly, but I am tired." Just then she yawned.

"Go to sleep," he said. "I'll wake you in ten minutes."

She thought about it, nodded, and said, "Okay, but make sure it's not any longer than that."

"No," he said. "I'll even set my watch for you."

She shifted, laid her head down, and let the sun take her under. At least she thought she was under. It seemed like two minutes and not ten minutes when he leaned across and patted her hand gently. She opened her eyes to find him right there, close to her, and she smiled. "Has it been ten minutes already?"

"It has, Sleeping Beauty," he said, his voice thick with emotions.

Something electric passed between the two of them. She reached out and gently stroked his cheek. "Thank you," she murmured. "I wouldn't want to get burned out here."

"Then I suggest we move our chairs so that we're in the shade now." And he drew back, breaking the moment.

The fact that the moment had even existed, that it was something now in her memory, something to smile about, something to cherish, was special all in itself. She got up, stretched, shifted the chaise longue so it sat in the shade, then looked at him and said, "Maybe we should move yours here too."

He nodded, shifted onto his good leg, and stood. This was the first she'd taken a good close-up look at his leg since his arrival here. It was all she could do to hold back her shock. But he must have noticed.

He looked at her face, looked down at his leg, and in a harsh voice said, "It's not very pretty, is it?" And he slammed himself back down onto the chair in the shade.

"It doesn't matter if anything's pretty about it or not," she said. "It's a marvel of human engineering."

Startled, he stared at her.

She looked at him with a flat expression on her face and said, "Did you expect me to be turning away in revulsion?"

He shrugged. "Yeah," he said. "I did. It's pretty ugly."

"I'm not so superficial," she said quietly. "A lot in life is ugly, but it doesn't mean that there isn't something good about it." She sat down in her chaise and studied his leg. "I mean, I just can't believe how much work they did to actually rebuild that leg for you. It must have been quite the process."

"Multiple surgeries. Some of the muscle off my buttocks, some off my back," he said. "It was kind of amazing. They took a little bit from my amputated foot and shin as well."

She studied both, seeing multiple scars. "It's still amazing," she said. "The fact is, that leg is functional, and it's definitely bigger than when I first saw you."

He looked at her, looked at his leg, and said, "Yeah?"

"Yeah," she said. "Did they take any measurements when you first arrived?"

He frowned, thought about it, and then slowly nodded. "I think they did. I just don't remember what the numbers were."

"Should be in your file somewhere, I'd think," she said. "They do that. They take measurements and weights to see how some of their patients handle surgeries and whether they're building up and getting stronger. And when the bone's involved, of course, the bone regrows around the damaged area. But with muscles, it's not quite the same process."

"No," he said. "And I'm getting more adjusted to the look of the leg."

"You should," she said. "Not only is it your leg and it's the one you've got and have been blessed to have, but it also looks more like a human leg now than a chicken leg." Her voice was cheerful, and she couldn't stop herself from bursting into laughter.

IAIN SETTLED BACK and studied her. "And that's what I meant earlier. Does it bother you?"

"No, it doesn't bother me," she said. "Except that I see the ingenuity of the human condition. I see the miracles of modern medicine. And I see the incredible courage of the human spirit. Don't ever be ashamed of that."

She stared directly into his eyes. "Hold your head high and ignore anybody who criticizes you. They haven't been through the wars, like you have. They don't have any right to the inner wounds and to the war wounds that you have. Wear them as badges of honor," she said. "And tell anyone else who makes a negative comment to stuff it."

He burst out laughing at that. "Out in the real world, I'd spend my entire day doing that some days."

She grinned. "I guess that's true. I just don't know why people have to be so mean. And why these mean people have time for that kind of crap."

"Exactly," he said with a laugh. "I certainly don't. I'm too busy trying to rebuild a life."

"Good," she said. "I'm really glad to hear that."

Chapter 12

SEVERAL DAYS LATER, with both of them slowly spending a bit more time together, she was sitting down alone for breakfast when Shane approached. She looked up, smiled, and said, "Hey, how is the boss?"

"Hardly the boss," he said, pulling out the chair and sitting down with a cup of coffee.

He looked tired. She frowned. "Are you spending too much time on your patients and forgetting to look after yourself?"

He looked up, then smiled, and said, "Well, I wouldn't have thought so, but it has been known to happen a time or two."

"Absolutely," she said. "How is Iain doing?"

"I was going to ask you that," he said in a teasing voice. "Seems like you two are really hitting it off."

"Maybe," she said. "I know he's got some issues, and I would like to see him get a little further down that path."

"Does his issue bother you?"

She shook her head and smiled. "No, but I don't want to hold him back either. I don't want him to be stopping short or shortchanging himself because I'm here." Shane stared at her in surprise, and she shrugged. "Just something I've been wondering about."

"Sounds like you need to shut off that part of your

brain," he said.

"Maybe," she said, "but he doesn't see his progress. I did ask if you guys had taken any measurements. And he said yes, but he didn't remember them. I told him to ask you about them. Or, at least if I didn't, he should." She laughed. "We get into such deep conversations that sometimes I forget what's been said."

"It's a good idea though," he said. "I was planning on taking more in the next few days anyway."

"Good," she said. "It might help him see that progress better."

He nodded. "What about you? You staying around now that you've been on the job what, four or five months?"

"I love it here," she said with a smile, "but it's not been quite three months, yet it seems like I've always been here."

He leaned forward and said, "And what if he leaves?"

She winced. "Right," she said. "That's not such a happy thought."

"Yet that's what we want for him."

She nodded slowly. "I guess it depends on what he ends up doing for himself."

"Exactly. And where," he said with a smile. He looked up and nodded toward the doorway. "Speaking of which, there he is."

She twisted, saw him, lifted a hand, and waved. "I guess those future discussions are something that might need to be discussed sooner than later."

"Something is there between you. It might help both of you if you could get a few of those details worked out."

She laughed. "Doesn't mean any of the details are ready to be worked out," she said.

"Maybe, but getting some of that stuff out of your head

will help you to not worry so much."

"Me or him?"

Shane stood as Iain approached. Shane looked at her with an insightful gaze and said, "How about for both of you?" And then he smiled at Iain and said, "Hey, Iain, how you doing?"

"Well, it's Tuesday. I made it through Monday," he said. "So, maybe we're doing okay."

"Maybe," Shane said. "We'll take a bunch of measurements here this Friday and see how your progress is doing."

Iain nodded. "That's a good idea," he said. "Maybe then I can see something tangible."

"Ah," Shane said with a smile. "Here I thought they were very tangible. But you're looking for data, aren't you?"

Iain shrugged. "Maybe," he said. "I hadn't realized how much I was looking for proof."

"Another very interesting and valid point," Shane said. "I'll see you later today." And he took off.

Iain sat down slowly, then put his crutches to the side.

She looked at the crutches and smiled and said, "You must be feeling better today."

"Tuesdays are often rough," he said. "After the weekend, Shane gets ahold of me on Monday and doesn't let go. On Tuesdays then, I tend to pay for it, but yesterday wasn't too bad."

"I think, like everything," she said, "it takes six weeks to get used to any routine. I'd sign up for a yoga course, and, for the first six weeks, that instructor would twist my body into a pretzel and force it into all kinds of movements, and I'd pay for it in pain for weeks. Then, all of a sudden, around six weeks, it'd be like my body would automatically form that pretzel without being forced into it, and I wouldn't have the pain afterward."

He chuckled. "Same for any new gym routine too," he admitted. "So maybe I'm finally adjusting to being here."

"How long has it been?"

"A couple months," he said easily. "But let's not forget I set myself back at the very beginning."

"Yes, you did," she said. "Doesn't matter though. There's no back. There's no right. There's no wrong. You're where you're at right now, and it sounds like maybe there is some progress."

"Maybe," he said. "Mentally as well. Thank you for that journal. I know I thanked you once, but I didn't really realize at the time how much it has helped. But it has."

"Good," she said. "I've barely taken the time to write in mine."

"I was wondering if you can get me a second one."

She stared at him in surprise, but, with a pleased smile, she nodded. "Absolutely. When do you need it?"

He shrugged. "I'm probably fine for the rest of this week."

That startled a laugh out of her. "That must be an interesting read."

"Nobody will read it," he said. "I plan to rip out all the pages and tear it apart afterward, maybe in a fire ceremony."

"I've heard that has helped a lot of people too," she said.

"It still feels a bit stupid though."

"It's not about feeling stupid. Remember?"

"I know," he said. "It's about doing what needs to be done. Getting my thoughts on paper."

"Exactly." She smiled and said, "Now I have to head to work."

"And I'll go get breakfast," he said with a laugh.

And that's the last she saw of him for a couple days. She did manage to get into town midweek and returned to the dollar store, but the same journal wasn't there anymore. Frowning, she headed to several other stores, but she wasn't impressed with those journals at all. She went to a discount store. As she wandered through, she asked one of the clerks. She took her to a large stationary section. There, she found two black journals. They weren't necessarily the same quality or the same type, and they were certainly double the price she'd paid last time, but she bought one for him.

As she headed back to Hathaway House, she put it on the seat beside her and drove all the way to her apartment. There, she grabbed Iain's newest journal and headed out for dinner, but she saw no sign of him. Frowning, she worried about that, but she ate her dinner and then headed down the hallway to his room.

When she knocked on his door, he called out, "Come in."

She opened the door and poked her head around. "Hey. You up for some company?"

He groaned. "I should be, but I'm pretty tired today."

She held out the journal and said, "I just wanted to give you this."

His face lit up. "Thanks," he said.

"It's the only color I could find," she said.

"Color doesn't matter," he said. "Now that I'm into this groove, I feel like I need to just keep pouring everything out."

"Understood," she said. And, with a smile, she turned and walked to the doorway. She stopped though and asked, "Did you get any dinner?"

He shook his head. "Honestly, I'm too tired."

"How about I pick you up something and bring it back?" He hesitated, and she shook her head. "Remember? I'm just being of service, like Dennis. It's not the same as having to ask for help."

"Hardly," he said, "but, ... if you could find me something simple, ... not too much though."

She nodded and headed back down, then snagged Dennis and told him that Iain was laid up in bed and asked if Dennis could put a plate together for Iain. And before long, she had a full tray. She was afraid it might be too much food, but he didn't have to eat it all, if that was the case. She made her way back and had left the door open so she could nudge it with her foot, then she headed inside and placed the tray down.

"You asleep?" she asked him softly. As his chest rose and fell, she realized he really had crashed on her. She went to lift the covers and realized he was holding the first journal open with his pen. She took the pen from his fingers, placed it down nearby, picked up the journal, and went to close it but caught sight of her name.

She warred with herself to not read it and then read one line that had been underlined, and it said, *Future uncertain.* Frowning, she quickly closed his journal, put it down on the table, pulled the covers up over his shoulders, and left. She closed the door behind her, wondering just what was going on in that mind of his. She really wanted to read his journal but knew that wasn't fair or right. It was intrusive and would probably just confuse the matter because, like he said, it had been ramblings, words that needed to get out of his head. But that mention of her was hard to let go of.

She headed back to her apartment, confused and more than a little worried about just what their future was.

IAIN WOKE THE next morning to see a tray of food sitting beside him and remembered asking her to get him something. "Crap," he said. He was covered in a blanket too, which meant that she'd returned with the food, covered him up, put his journal and pen to the side, and left him here. He sighed and shifted his body, wondering at just how tired he really was. He'd made all sorts of progress last night as he had sifted through some of his feelings of insecurity and failure from his childhood.

They weren't even big issues, but they were momentous enough for him to remember, and he'd worked hard at releasing them and forgiving everybody involved, including himself. Now he just felt fairly emotionally overwrought. He got up and managed a hot shower. And, by the time he was dressed, he was feeling fine but emotionally tired. He made his way to and in his wheelchair and headed to breakfast.

As soon as he saw him, Dennis asked how was dinner.

He shook his head. "I'm sorry," he said. "I was asleep when Robin brought it back."

Dennis nodded. "I'll collect the tray later," he said. "Sleep is always the best answer."

Iain realized he should have brought it back with him. "And I was obviously too tired this morning to think about bringing the tray back myself," he said. "I'm sorry. I could have saved you a trip."

"Have to get my exercise somehow," Dennis said with a big smile. With that, he served up breakfast and carried it over to the deck to eat. By the time Iain was done and made it to his first appointment, Shane was sitting at the computer, waiting for him.

"We'll run through a bunch of tests and do a progress report," Shane said. "It's been eight weeks since you've been here, so it's perfect timing." He quickly took a bunch of measurements from Iain's legs, waist, hips, and had him stand. Then he took a bunch of photographs, the same ones that he had done as part of his initial intake analysis and then, when he sat him down, Shane said, "So let's go through some of these."

"Is there anything to go through?" Iain asked.

"There definitely is," Shane said. "Take a look." And there in the file were his stats.

Iain realized that his thigh—his chicken thigh—had gained three and a half inches in bulk around the top of the thigh and a good two inches around the base of it. He stared at that data in shock. He looked down at his leg and said, "You know what? Robin did say something about my thigh looking a lot better now, but I hadn't seen it."

"Well, this'll help," Shane said. And he brought up two pictures side by side on the monitor.

Iain stopped, stared, sucked his breath back, and went, "Wow."

"Now you look me in the eye and tell me," Shane said, "when you look at these two pictures of your thigh—when you first arrived and your thigh now, today—has there been any progress?"

Something inside had broken free, something needing to crack and to collapse around him, releasing something he didn't quite understand. But he could feel hope. He could feel a sense of life and a sense of something inside himself bursting free as he stared at those images. He smiled a huge grateful smile, a beaming smile. "I don't know how you did it," he said, "but that's not just progress. That's incredible progress." Shane lifted a high five, and Iain slapped it hard and said, "Whoa, can we repeat that?"

"I fully intend to," Shane said. "I think it's important that you take a look at this." And he opened another folder he had on his desk, then held up two pictures. One was a mangled-up leg, and one was a healthy, strong leg.

"And whose are those?"

"Another patient who was here about six months ago," he said. "This was his before, and this was his after photo."

Iain stared at them, and he could feel tears in his eyes. "Why didn't you show me that when I first arrived?"

"Because it was too far in the future for you to fully grasp," he said. "But now that you can see this much progress in your own body, I can make sure that you get this as your end result."

And, for that, Iain would give anything. "If you can do that," he said, "you're a miracle worker."

Shane grinned. "Not me," he said. "*You*. I don't do this. *You* do this."

Chapter 13

MAYBE ROBIN HAD picked up something from Iain's mood, but it seemed like her life was off today too. When Dani called her into her office at the end of the day, Robin was surprised and worried. As she walked in, she sat down with a hard *thump*. "Problems?"

Dani looked up at her in surprise and then laughed. "I'm so sorry," she said. "No, there's absolutely no problem." She shook her head. "I keep forgetting that I'm the boss, and often people get nervous when I ask to speak with them."

"Especially when we've had such a hard week downstairs," Robin explained. "Stan is beside himself with all the paperwork."

Immediately Dani frowned. "Does he need help down there?"

"I don't think so. We've got one of the gals on holiday, and she handles most of the bookkeeping."

Dani rolled her eyes. "We all need holidays, but covering for people off on holidays can be a real pain."

"So, is there a reason why you called me up?"

She laughed. "There is. I wanted to ask you a personal question." She hesitated and looked at the door. "You mind shutting the door, please?"

Robin hopped up, closed the door, sat back down again, and said, "Does this have something to do with Iain?"

Dani's eyebrows rose. "Direct. I like that," she said. "Yes, it does."

"I hope it's okay that we formed a friendship," Robin said anxiously. "I never honestly gave it a thought."

"It absolutely is okay," Dani said reassuringly. "The only time I intervene is if I can see that it's slowing down or completely stopping one of the patient's healing. As long as everything is moving forward, then I don't have any objection."

"Is there a problem with Iain?"

"No," she said. "I think he's had a breakthrough."

"Well, that would be wonderful," Robin said emphatically. "And I think it's long overdue."

Dani's eyebrows rose. "Tell me more."

Then, suddenly realizing that she was talking about Iain behind his back, Robin sank into her chair and said, "I'd rather not. It feels odd."

"Understood," Dani said. "As much as I'd like to know what you know, I do respect that you don't want to talk about him. I just wondered how serious it was on your part."

"I don't know," Robin said. "We haven't got that far, but I really like him."

"Good," Dani said. "According to Shane, you seem to be a strong motivator for Iain."

"And I guess that's a good thing, providing we're all on the same page."

"Exactly," Dani said with half a smile. "Which is why I'm asking how serious it is on your part. I'd hate to see him have a setback anywhere in the next six weeks while we sort out how far he can actually go."

"But neither do I want to be something that I'm not in order to keep his progress going," Robin said slowly. "So I guess it's a good thing that I really like the man, huh?"

Dani burst into a bright and light laughter, filling the room and spreading beyond. Robin had spent a fair bit of time with Dani since she'd arrived here but never really on a one-to-one basis. People were always around Dani. Robin really liked the woman and loved her heart. "I'll tell you one of the odd things about Iain was we get into these really philosophical questions," she said. "Or maybe more like New Age healing kind of questions. I bought him some journals to write in."

"I saw those," Dani said in surprise. "I wondered where he'd gotten them. Of course everybody is allowed to have stuff like that, but often I offer journals for people, if they need them."

"Well, the first one," Robin said, "I just picked up at the dollar store, and he filled that one fairly quickly, which really surprised me. So then I got him a second one."

"It's a lovely gift," Dani said warmly. "It's not just the gift itself but it's the opening up of a doorway that allows somebody to help heal his own problems."

"I thought it might help him. Me too. In a way, I'm used to being alone, and I find that sometimes interacting with somebody on a personal level makes me feel awkward," she tried to explain.

"A long time since your last relationship?"

"Yes, certainly. A few months before I came here," she said. "And definitely a relationship that wasn't healthy. So I was grateful for a chance to leave and to get a start fresh."

"As long as starting fresh isn't ..." And then her voice fell away.

Robin nodded. "As long as starting fresh isn't trying to hide, you mean?"

Dani nodded with relief in her eyes. "Yes," she said. "Then I realized how personal I was being, and it wasn't my job to poke at you."

At that, Robin started to chuckle. "Versus poking at the patients here?"

"Exactly," Dani said. "You're not one of the patients coming here to grow and to learn."

"But I don't see how anybody can't grow and learn while here," she said. "Just so much healing is going on around us that it's almost impossible to stay unaffected."

"Exactly," she said. "But, in an odd way, sometimes you can become dulled to it because there's just so much of it. We see the same thing over and over again. Yet it's always different. It always has a different face, always has a bit of a different twist, as it's individualized per patient. But you become almost accepting that it's happening, and then you become blasé about it."

"Maybe for you," Robin said. "I haven't been here that long or had the same interactions that you have had. I deal with the animals downstairs, and it often amazes me just how much healing they accomplish all on their own, without any of this head stuff. Whereas we humans make life so difficult and so complicated. If we could get out of our own heads, our bodies know exactly what to do."

Dani stopped, stared at her for a long moment, and then nodded. "I agree completely," she said. "It's one of the reasons I love my horses, and I love the freedom of when they can just run and go for miles. Sometimes I used to do that to get away from my problems and my troubles, whereas the horses didn't seem to have that same issue. They just ran because it was beautiful to run, and it felt good. It was freeing, and they loved the sensation. I loved it too, but, for me, it was more—at the time—a case of needing to get away. Now I ride because I'm in the same space as the horses. I love the freedom it offers me and just the sense of enjoying the wind in my face and their muscles underneath my legs." She gave her a smile.

"Iain misses horses," she said abruptly.

Dani stopped, looked at her, and then gave a clipped nod. "I think I remember something about that from when he first arrived." She shuffled papers on her desk. "We could also talk to him about doing some horse therapy."

"I think he would absolutely love anything that would get him back to horses, even if it just means going out for a couple hours."

"Has someone told him that he's allowed to be down there at the stables or in the outlying pastures?" Dani asked with a frown.

"I'm not sure," Robin said. "I think it would be a wonderful gift for him."

"Maybe I'll go talk to him now," Dani said. "I've got a bunch of other horses coming in. They're traveling through the countryside and needed a place to unload to give the horses a rest from the long trip."

"Well, that will be nice. Are they friends of yours?" she asked curiously.

"Yes, they are," she said. "I've got twelve gooseneck trailers coming in, hauling up to forty-eight show horses."

Robin's jaw dropped.

Dani laughed. "There'll be quite a few horses to see, if you're around this weekend," she said. "Obviously we need to be extra careful. The horses are allowed to have their own space, but I'll be moving all our animals over at least one or two pastures." At this, she looked out her window, as if she

DALE MAYER

hadn't decided exactly what she would do yet. "But I think maybe, if Iain's around, we can get him down, at least in the wheelchair, where he can visit with the horses a little bit."

"I'm sure he'd love that. I caught him out with Hoppers on the lawn here not too long ago," she said with a laugh. "He just wanted to see Hoppers out of his cage and running free for a bit."

"And, whether he knows it or not, that's synonymous with how he feels himself," Dani said with a smile. "Thanks for reminding me about his love of horses. I'll see if I can come up with something."

"I don't know if he's seen any of the progress that we all see yet," Robin said, "but if he has, maybe as a reward?"

"Interesting," Dani said. "Rewards are something that we try not to hand out because we think every day showing up for the rehab deserves a reward, and, therefore, very quickly they almost become meaningless. But maybe as a treat."

"Same diff," she said. "Not quite, I know, but it does effectively address what I was hoping for."

"Let me see if I can swing this so soon," she said. "It'll be a busy weekend, so I don't know if I can make anything happen at this point."

"Not necessary either," Robin said, standing up. "Just nice to know that maybe he can make some time for himself down there."

IAIN HAD TO admit he was feeling incredibly emboldened and hopeful after his Friday afternoon session with Shane. He'd gone looking for Robin to share the good news. She had been super-excited, even though she had already seen his progress that day by the pool. They'd had dinner together, and then he'd kind of crashed, his energy cycling downward, and she'd left him at his room soon afterward. Now, it was Saturday morning, and he heard sounds of large vehicles pulling in. It surprised him, and he got up and got dressed, then made his way out in his wheelchair onto the deck of the cafeteria and watched as several huge horse trailers came in.

Dennis came up to his side. "Dani is up to it again," he said with a big smile. He handed Iain a cup of coffee. "You'll need this."

"What's going on?" he asked.

"A large group of show horses are moving across the state," he said. "Dani offered a couple pastures today and tonight, for the horses to get out of the trailers. They can only travel so many hours before they need to be let out again."

"Wow," Iain said. And in a nice and orderly fashion, all of the big trucks and trailers pulled up beside each other.

Dani was already there, talking to the drivers, and she was opening up pastures. And before long, at least forty horses were unloaded and moved into the fields. Two were pastures, several cross-fenced, and the horses immediately took to the grass, which was pretty high, some eating, and some kicking it up, dancing to be out of the trailers.

He stared in amazement. "Dani's heart is really big, isn't it?"

"The biggest," he said. "Anytime she can help others, she does, particularly when it comes to animals."

"I wish I could be down there," he said.

"I don't know if the actual trucks will stay around. I imagine some will head into town. This is for the horses and not so much for the people," Dennis said with a laugh. "At least I haven't been given any instructions that I'll have an extra thirty-six-odd people today."

A note of worry was present in his voice, and Iain looked up at him and laughed. "Would it matter to you if you did?"

Dennis thought about it, shrugged, and said, "Nah, we always have leftovers anyways."

Iain nodded. "That's what I expected," he said. "It seems like there's always lots of food at your table."

The two men continued to watch the horses, and, sure enough, several of the vehicles filled up with people and disconnected from the trailers and headed back out of the parking lots again. Some were staying, and it looked like four people were hanging around to keep an eye on the animals. Which, considering the amount of horse flesh out there, made a lot of sense. And yet, for all Iain could see, a lot more than four were needed to mind some forty horses.

At one point in time, he saw Dani looking up in his direction. He waved to her, and she waved enthusiastically back. Within about ten minutes, she marched toward him, standing under the deck. "Do you want to come see them?" she asked, her face alight with joy and excitement.

He hesitated. "Do you think the wheelchair will spook them? I don't have my crutches with me."

"Nah," she said. "These guys have been flown all over the world. They're used to all kinds of travel, including scooters and wheelchairs."

He nodded. "I'll head down the elevator and come out the bottom."

"I'll walk with you," she said and met him soon afterward. "Have you had any experience with horses?"

"Lots," he said, "when I was younger. I haven't ridden

since my accident."

"Well, you might go for a ride today, if you want," she said. "I probably have to give Shane a call first though."

"Well, how about you don't call Shane," he said, "and you let me go for the ride anyway?"

She stared at him for a long moment. "How's your back?"

"The back is pretty good. The leg is much better," he said, and he shared the results from Shane's progress report.

"Now that," she said in delight, "is awesome."

"I know," he said. "That's what I was thinking. So, horseback riding would be lovely."

As they walked outside, Robin walked toward them. She was laughing. "Dani, when you said horses were coming, I didn't realize you meant *horses* were coming. I know you said how many but that didn't compute until I actually saw them altogether."

Iain looked at her and said, "Did Dani tell you?"

"Only that she'd offered up pasture for horses to have a spot to run around after being transported," she said. They walked up to one of the gates and just stood and stared at the horses, beautiful chestnuts and palominos and every color under the sun as they moved through the pasture. Some were running; some were kicking up their heels, happy to be out; and some were immediately head down in the grass, and even two were lying down.

"Aren't they beautiful?" Robin said.

"Do you know how to ride?" Dani asked.

Robin shook her head. "City girl all my life," she said. "No opportunity. This was a rich kid's sport."

"Or a poor kid's sport," Dani said, laughing. "I used to ride because I mucked out the stalls, and that was my job."

"I hear you," she said. "We didn't even have horse barns around."

"Interesting." They moved along the pasture with several horses coming over to talk to them, and two of the men came over, shaking hands with Dani.

"You've got a hell of a setup here, Dani," Wesley said.

She nodded. "It's been a long haul to get here, but I'm sure you can understand the joy to be in this position now."

"Absolutely," he said. He looked over at Iain and reached out to shake his hand. "I'm Wesley," he said. "Six of these horses are mine."

"I'm Iain," he said. "One of Dani's current residents upstairs."

"I'm Robin, one of the vet techs who works at the vet clinic downstairs."

The men turned to look at the main building and nodded. "We've heard Dani's done incredible things here."

"Well, I can attest to that," Iain said quietly. "I just had a progress report yesterday, and I'm amazed."

"That's what we like to hear," he said. "I got a nephew who's in bum shape, just returned from Afghanistan. They thought he would come back in a pine box, but he's still kicking."

"When he's ready," Dani said quietly, "send me his name and file, and we'll see if we can get him in."

The man's face worked up with emotion, and he nodded. "Thanks," he said. "I don't know what it costs, but it's not a price any of us have a problem paying if it gets the boy back on his feet."

"Exactly why I do what I do and why our donations are so important," she said. "Because unfortunately a heavy cost is involved in doing this, but it's fairly amazing when you think about just what we can do. And how far these kids and men," she said, with a nod toward Iain, "come. That leg of his was pretty much useless, but he has done very well now."

Just then Stan came out to join them, looking a little bit rough.

"Stan, you haven't had your coffee yet," Dani said with a smile.

"Sure haven't," he said. "But I wouldn't miss a chance to see this many horses all at once." He reached out and shook hands with the two men, then introduced himself as the vet for Hathaway House's animal clinic.

The men nodded and one said, "You've got a great reputation here too."

"Well, if I do," he said, "it's based on a lot of hard work and a lot of heart."

"That it is," one of the men said. "Anybody who works with animals has got to have a lot of heart."

Stan looked at Iain and said, "You have experience with horses, don't you?"

"Yeah," he said, "but not since my accident."

"I'm pretty sure Midnight would let you go for a ride, if you want to give it a try."

"I'd love to," he said, "but what I don't want to do is set back my own healing."

Dani nodded, pulled out her phone, stepped away a few steps, and made a call. Stan stepped forward and said, "I've got a western saddle around here," he said. "I doubt you do English, do you?"

Iain chuckled. "No, my experience is cowboy style," he said. "Give me a western saddle or even bareback." But then, he thought about it and said, "Or maybe not bareback at this point. But, man, I'd love to get back to riding."

"Bareback is hard on the butt," Stan complained. "I can ride well enough," he said, "but horses like this, well, they're just so superb," he murmured in delight as they all stared out at the massive pastures thriving with the visiting horses. Even Appie and Lovely, Midnight and the others, like Molly, had walked over to visit with the new arrivals.

One of the two men looked over and asked, "Is that a llama?"

"She is," Stan said. "She was a rescue and came with Appie the Appaloosa. The two of them have been together since they were born."

"Got to love that," the man said. "I've got a goat at home that won't be separated from my dog. I used to take the dog everywhere but that also meant I had to take the goat. So I leave them both at home now." He shook his head. "The bonds that animals make is just amazing."

"That it is," Stan said. "That it is."

Dani came back a few minutes later and said, "I just talked to Shane, and he says, if you'll just walk the horse on the field—no trotting, no jogging, no galloping—he's all for you getting on the back of a horse."

Iain looked up at her, hope in his eyes, and said, "Seriously?" He looked over at Stan and back at Dani and said, "But do you have a western saddle that might fit?"

"Absolutely," she said. She put her fingers in her mouth and turned toward Midnight and let out a sharp whistle. Midnight's head and ears came up, and he came galloping across the pasture toward her. All the men watched as she walked to the gate and opened it up. Midnight immediately walked out, and she brought him to where Iain was.

"You don't need to put lead on him?"

"No. He knows exactly where he belongs," she said with

a laugh. "Give me about ten minutes, and I'll have him dressed up." She walked with him back to the barn on the side of the pastures at the back. And, while they watched, she threw on a blanket, tossed up a saddle, and put a bridle on his head. With a bit in his mouth, she carefully draped the reins over his back and then walked with Midnight at her side, joining them once more. "The only thing that I don't know," she said, "is how to get you up there."

"Depends on the stirrup length," he said. "And I might manage to get up from a fence post." He stood up on his one leg and said, "I wish I had my crutches right now."

"I'll go get them," Robin said, and she disappeared.

"If I can help, let me know," one of the two men said, stepping forward.

Iain looked at him. He was big enough. He was about his height. "If you can give me a hand to get over to that fence," he said, "I think I can hop up a couple slats and just slide over onto Midnight's back." And, with a stranger's arm around his back, Iain managed to make his way to the fence. There, he climbed up to the top by hopping. Dani led Midnight to him. And, grabbing the pommel, he slid over to the horse's back and sat astride Midnight. The horse shifted ever-so-slightly under his weight, and he put his good leg into the stirrup and then chuckled. "This must be your saddle, Dani. Look at the stirrups."

She laughed because his stump was almost the right size for her stirrups. She walked around and quickly lowered the other stirrup and said, "That's about all I can do on this saddle. I guess I need to find a half dozen more for patients, don't I?"

"This is your horse though," he said. And with a gentle *click* and a nudge of his knee, Midnight shifted forward slightly, but waited for Dani to return. Dani walked to the pasture she'd come out of and opened the gate.

She had a second halter in her hand. "Am I riding your saddle?"

"Yep," she said. She called out to a different horse, and the mare came walking over.

He said, "That one looks like I should be on her, just in case."

"Nope," she said. She tossed the halter up and around, put the bit into the horse's mouth, and, with a smooth movement, hopped onto the back of the mare's withers. At the nudge of her knee, she said, "Let's go for a walk." With Stan and everyone else standing behind at the closed gate, she led Midnight up and around the pasture at a gentle walk.

Iain walked carefully, waiting to see if his hips jarred his back. When he realized the pain was not hitting him every time the horse walked, he settled in. As he settled in, the horse's gait also smoothed out.

"Good," she said. "Midnight is doing just fine. How are you?"

"Well, he's doing fine because I've now calmed down," he said with a pleased smile. "This is truly a gift. I never thought in my best days that I'd ever get on the back of a horse again."

"Well, I sure don't want you out here working and roping calves," she said. "But, as a horse lover, I can certainly relate to it being something you strive to get back to."

"And how," he said. He turned his face up to the sun. "Just even knowing that I'm out here …"

"I know," she said. "I completely understand."

And he could hear the catch in her voice and knew that she really did. They were out for an hour, and he could feel his back muscles twitching. He looked at her and said, "As much as I don't want to stop ..."

"I was about to suggest we go back. Shane said no more than an hour anyway."

"And that was probably a tad too long anyway," he said. "But I don't care. This was truly a momentous day, and I thank you so much for the honor." He leaned forward and gently rubbed Midnight on his big neck, threading his fingers through the silky black mane. "This is your personal horse, isn't he?"

"Yes," she said. "He and I have been together since he was a colt."

"And he's blessed," Iain said. "We don't always have friendships like this."

"No, but you have a friend who drove you from the VA hospital to here. And he did it against his better judgment, and he did it because it's what you wanted to do," she said quietly. "So I wonder if you realize just how hard that was for him."

And then he remembered how he hadn't texted Bruce back. He groaned. "I seem to have forgotten so many things that are really important in life lately," he said.

She chuckled. "You know what? You're not alone in that. It's something that happens on a regular basis to a lot of men here. I don't know why, but it's like, as they move forward in one aspect of their life—and in this case it's the focus on your healing or strengthening your body and getting your movement back—so much else falls by the wayside. I have found that, no matter who the people, they tend to be very forgiving because they know that what you're doing here is super important and takes extreme focus."

"But who said that kind of focus," he said, "meant dropping everything else? Bruce was my best friend for so long, and I haven't yet told him about my progress."

"Well, I have my cell phone," she said. "Do you want me to take a couple pictures?"

He grinned. "I so do." And, with that, as they walked, she took several photographs of him on Midnight. By the time they made it back to the gathered crowd, Midnight backed up to the side of the fence. It was all Iain could do to swing his partial leg over the fence and step onto the railing as he swung his right leg over. He managed to hop down and stand against the fence, but his good leg was trembling. He had a four-foot climb to get back to where the wheelchair was parked. He knew he really needed to make it, but, boy, it looked a hell of a long way away.

Wesley stepped up and said, "I'm here to help."

Iain looked up at him, smiled, and said, "And I'll accept that help. Thank you."

And, with that, the other man gently assisted Iain up the short distance, until he could sit back down in the wheelchair. When he collapsed, he groaned and said, "I so wanted to do that with crutches, but ..."

"One of the things I've learned in life," Wesley said, "is you got to take everything one bite at a time. You can't eat a massive smorgasbord at once, but you can take one bite, enjoy it, and then have another bite and enjoy it. This is a journey, and, for you, it's likely to be the only journey you ever need to have in this direction. So, I get that you want to reach the end as fast as possible, but don't forget to take the journey in small bites and to enjoy each and every one."

Chapter 14

TEARS WERE IN Robin's eyes, and she kept wiping them back. But she reached down and gripped Iain's shoulder from behind him. Almost without thinking, he reached up and laced his fingers with hers, and the two just hung on to each other. She was overwhelmed with emotions. The joy on his face when she'd seen him out there on the horse, seeing his body hold him and giving him that moment of joy, she knew that this was just a starting point to even more emotional and joy-filled moments. The fact that he'd gotten on a horse and had made it an hour out there was absolutely phenomenal.

And she knew that, no matter what else he tried to do now, he'd do just fine. He was a special man. He'd gone through so much, and here she was, the one who was not doing as well. And she didn't have any valid reason not to. And she was desperate for him to do well, and, at the same time, she also knew that it could mean he'd move on and move past her. She gripped his fingers even harder, and, when she tried to release his hand, he wouldn't let her go. She smiled and said, "I don't know about you, but I haven't had breakfast."

He looked up at her, then smiled and said, "No, I haven't either."

And, with that, the crowd started to disperse. He'd been

so happy and so proud, as if he'd finally succeeded at something. She walked beside him, her hand still on his shoulder, even as he needed both his hands to push his wheelchair toward the elevator. She could feel the stress in his back with each shove forward. "You know that I could push you," she said hesitantly.

"No. Carry the crutches," he said. "We'll go back to my room and put those away and then head for lunch, if that's okay with you."

"Definitely okay with me," she said. Stan had gone somewhere. She presumed he was still talking with the others, but she knew Iain needed to go relax. "Unless you need to lie down."

"I'll have a nap this afternoon," he said, "but I want to eat out on the deck and watch the horses."

"That we can do." They made their way to his room, where she put away his crutches, and then, walking back at his side, headed over to the cafeteria. A noisy crowd was in the center of it. She looked at him and said, "Do you want me to get food for both of us, while you claim a table out in the sun?"

He hesitated.

She looked at him and said, "There's no need to not accept help again."

"I seem to be bad at that," he said. Then he nodded. "If you wouldn't mind," he said. "We will have to compete for a table out on the deck."

"Go," she said. "Get us one, and I'll come join you in a few minutes." She watched as he headed out, completely okay to do that, and realized just how far he'd come. As she got into line, she grabbed two trays. Dennis was once again at the forefront, serving and talking to everybody as they came by.

He looked at her, smiled, and said, "I saw Iain on the horse."

"Did you see him?" she said with a beaming smile. "That was one happy man."

"And he should be," Dennis said. "He's a good guy." He looked at the food and said, "But I bet he's really hungry now, isn't he?"

"Hungry and very tired," she said. "Not that he'll admit to the last part though."

At that, Dennis chuckled. "No, of course he won't," he said. "That would make life too easy. Men are complex."

"Nah," she said teasingly. "Women are complex. Men are simple."

He beamed a grin at her. "You could be right," he said. "Men just want the basic needs."

"What's that?" she asked. "Beer, ribs, and football?" Several of the men around her cracked grins. Dennis waved a finger at her admonishingly.

She laughed and said, "Good food. He definitely needs good food."

"Well, I've got all kinds of it here today. What would you like?"

She quickly made choices for both of them, with Dennis loading up their plates, and knew she couldn't carry both trays if she loaded them too heavily. So, she put one by the coffee area, carried one out, and then came back and got the other one. By the time she was done, they were both sitting on one side together, the table pushed up against the railing so they could see as much as they could. Iain ate slowly, but his gaze was on the horses.

"I think an awful lot could be done with horses, don't

you?" she asked him.

"Some friends of mine back in New Mexico," he said, "they formed a new company to help veterans get employed, to find a second career, even to build suitable housing for returning vets. I sent one of them an email a while ago, wondering what all their operation did. I haven't even checked to see if he has responded yet."

"And then what?"

"Then," he said. "I was wondering about setting up something like what they have done—but here."

She looked at him in surprise, but something warm and caring wrapped around her heart like a hug. "So, you're thinking about staying close?"

He looked at her, smiled, and said, "That's where you are, isn't it?"

She nodded slowly. "Yes," she said. "That is definitely where I am."

"In that case," he said, "yes, I'm looking at staying somewhere close. We still have a ways to go on this journey of ours, but I'm sure not ready to call it quits." Just then, shouts of laughter came from behind him, interrupting their conversation. He looked at her, smiled, and said, "Eat. We'll talk later."

"Sounds good," she said. And they proceeded to dig into lunch, but her heart was full, and her soul was happy.

IAIN SHOULDN'T HAVE said anything about his plans because he really didn't have any plans; it was more a vague dream. But he'd been emboldened by the horseback ride. He looked at her and said, "It might not work out."

"What might not work out?"

"If I do decide to do something like that."

"It's an idea," she said in surprise. "Ideas are just that. I hope something like that does happen for you. I think you would find a great deal of personal satisfaction in helping others get established."

He nodded slowly. "That's what I was thinking. I know these guys in New Mexico. They've done so much good for other people. I was just thinking it might be nice to do something like that myself."

"So, work toward it," she said. "You're probably not capable of doing it all yet, but that doesn't mean in a few months you won't be."

"After today," he said, "it does feel like I've made some major strides. I'm not there yet, but I'm getting there."

"Is there anything else that you want to work toward?"

"Unless I wake up tomorrow morning," he said jokingly, "and I think this is a terrible idea."

She looked at him steadily. "And, if it is a terrible idea," she said, "maybe what you need to do is look at why you suddenly feel that way. Because it sure doesn't sound like a terrible idea to me."

"Maybe," he said. "Maybe I'll spend some time with that journal and dig a little deeper."

She gave him a fat smile. "You do that."

"And you," he challenged. "What about your journal?"

"I haven't even started," she admitted.

"Well, while I work in mine, you do something for yourself," he said with a smile. "It'd be nice if we both move forward together."

"It would, wouldn't it?" she said. "I need to work on a couple things definitely, so maybe I should."

"No," he said. "Not *maybe*. We've made a lot of progress together. Let's keep that up."

She smiled, then nodded and said, "I can work with that."

"Good," he said. "Now, I hate to ask, but how do you feel about getting us some coffee?"

She chuckled. "I can do that too."

Chapter 15

ROBIN WAS HAPPY that, for the next few weeks, it seemed like there was steady progress. At least on his part. She tried to open that journal because it had been her idea after all. But, every time she did, that blank page just stared back at her, daring her to mark it up. If she really wanted this relationship with Iain to work, she knew she had garbage she should let go of. Everybody did, right?

She could feel the frustration building inside her. She didn't know what she was supposed to do about it and went through the day's motions with a smile plastered on her face. But inside, she held this knowing worry that just maybe, maybe Iain was better off to go forward and to leave her because she hadn't done her work. Maybe she didn't have any pressing work to do, but it just meant that he was that much more progressive about his life, and she felt like she needed to at least have something to offer of herself.

The days were busy and packed with animals coming and going, and, at the end of Wednesday, when she collapsed on her back on the grass outside the vet clinic, propped up on her elbows, and just stared at the pastures and the horses, it seemed like the weekend with the show horses was a long time ago. It had only been two days long, yet still one of the major events that Iain talked about. And she was so happy for him. At the same time though, it left her feeling empty on the inside. She groaned out loud.

"That doesn't sound very positive," Dani's cheerful voice broke through her reverie.

Robin sat up slowly and looked at her. "It's been a rough couple days," she admitted.

Dani nodded. "I hear you. It's been busy upstairs too."

"Still," she said, "what you did for Iain was huge."

"And yet you appear bothered, like something is not quite right," Dani said. She slipped the halter off Midnight, plunked the saddle down on the ground in such a way that it seemed to rest upon air, and walked over closer. "Everything okay between the two of you?"

"Yes," Robin said. "It's just that I feel like he's doing so much and making progress in leaps and bounds ..."

"And you feel like you're supposed to be doing something to keep up with him?"

She shrugged. "When you put it that way, it sounds stupid."

"It is stupid," Dani said. "It's not a competition."

"I know that," she said. "I don't feel competitive. That feels wrong. But it also feels like I should be doing some prep work myself."

Dani looked at her for a long moment. "Where's this coming from?"

"Inside," Robin said instantly. "It was my idea to buy the journals. I thought that maybe I had some issues to work on."

"Remember that you can only work on things when you're ready to work on them," Dani said slowly. "No good can come from pushing something like that."

"But what if I don't quite get there?" she asked. "Or are we back to the fact that things have to happen in the right time?"

"What makes you think anything's broken inside?" Dani asked. She squatted in front of Robin. "You seem well-adjusted. You're healthy. You haven't been tossing yourself at every man who comes by. You've picked somebody stable and steady and who has a wonderful spirit," she said warmly. "Why is it you feel like you need to be working on you?"

"Because everybody has something to work on," she said.

"I get that," Dani said. "We all have issues. We all have childhood traumas. We all have resentments, and we all feel guilty for something. But again, those aren't things that you can just pull out and say, *Today I'll deal with this.* A trigger usually happens, that sets off something, and then you grab it and say, *Okay, now that you've shown me the light, I'm dealing with it.*"

"And in the meantime?"

"Maybe you should be asking yourself why you feel like you need to do this."

"You're right. I need to be doing something for myself."

"Or what?" Dani asked, still prodding.

She took a deep breath and said, "Or I'm not as good as him."

Dani's eyebrows shot up. "So, it's not a case of being in a competition but suffering a judgment?"

"No," Robin said, shaking her head. Then she stopped and said, "Well, kind of." Confusion filtered through her. "I don't know what I'm saying," she cried out.

"And that's the issue facing you right now," Dani said. "Forget about all your history. What you need to work out is why you feel that you need to be working on you in order to catch up to or to be as good as Iain."

And, with that, she grabbed her saddle and walked toward the barn, leaving Robin sitting in the grass, staring out at the pastures all around her. Is that what this was all about? Because, in her logical mind, she knew that was garbage. But, inside her heart of hearts, she did wonder if maybe, maybe she wasn't as good as him. She wasn't applying herself as hard or as effectively as he was. He hadn't seen any progress and figured there wasn't any to have, and then, all of a sudden, he'd come up with all kinds of progress. Would it be the same for her? And why is it that she felt like she needed to have that same kind of progress? She hadn't been through anywhere near the trauma he had.

Confused and wearing herself out emotionally, she got up and slowly walked to her apartment. She had a shower to help relieve some of the stress still settling on her shoulders, and, rather than going out and grabbing food, she grabbed her journal and sat outside in her small rear patio. She opened a bottle of sparkling water and sat in the shade and wrote down some of the words that Dani had said. As she started, her pen picked up and moved faster and faster and faster. By the time she finally drained her brain of whatever rolled around in there, she had to shake her hand out from cramping.

But inside, she was elated. Because *this* was what she had wanted. She had had her breakthrough. However, somewhere in her stream of consciousness rambling was the *something underneath* that consequently had to be worked on. She glanced through her writing, hoping to read whatever were the important parts, hoping she could still decipher her own writing done so fast and so sloppily.

The main question was, *Why did she feel not good enough?*

Granted, her ex made her feel less than, but even now, not a full year later, she already knew that their relationship was not healthy, was not right, was not good for either of them. So she felt like she had a handle on that event. Yet the same thing was coming up now with Iain. Why did she think she was not good enough for him? Why this recurring judgment?

Robin had previously thought something in her present situation was the trigger, which trigger issue Dani had brought up earlier today.

It wasn't Robin's present situation at issue at all. It was her past. Her response just kept recurring, like with her ex, like now with Iain. That was her underlying problem that she needed to address right now. Because she knew one thing for sure. Iain would be quite unhappy if he thought his breakthroughs and recent successes were the trigger to finding where her current problem issue lay.

But the fact of the matter was, she had been working on the exact same issue inside her that Iain had been dealing with here at Hathaway House: feeling the pressure to succeed, seeing others' successes, and not having some of it and yet wanting it.

Instead, for Robin, a whole other issue lay beyond that had to be reopened and dealt with.

As she stared at the words on the page, she realized how absolutely incredibly stupid it all was. Iain would be angry to think that she was feeling less than him because he'd finally started to make progress. To Iain, there was no downside to his recent successes. He would be hurt to hear that from her. *From her*, who was standing beside him in so many ways, but … wasn't really happy for him? Even she ached when she thought that.

But she knew that wasn't the truth. She didn't want to derail him, and she sure didn't want to disappoint him. She had to fix this. *Now.*

Right now.

And, in fact, it was almost conceited, arrogant of herself. He'd been through so much and had survived and done so well, something that she knew she couldn't have done even half as well as he had. And she'd been sympathetic and wanting him to get that same breakthrough. So was this all talk and no real heartfelt sentiment?

Then, as soon as he made major strides at really healing himself, she had immediately felt less than him. She shook her head, wondering where all this came from. Then she had reached back, far back into her life, pinpointing a couple times in her childhood where a judgment, then a grief—or was it vice versa?—had overwhelmed her senses.

She found it in her rambling writings. *Like when her mother had passed away. Like when her brother had been kicked out of the house at sixteen, leaving Robin alone with her father and his new wife.*

At the time, Robin's grief had warred with her anger and her judgment and had left Robin feeling like *Robin* wasn't important enough for her mother to stick around. It made no sense. Not to the adult and grown-up Robin. Her mother didn't choose to die. Her mother didn't choose to leave Robin and Keith. Yet her mother's death felt that way to Robin back then as a child—and maybe to an extent still did. How sad was that?

Her brother and father had never got along, and she knew Keith had been just as devastated when their mother had passed away. Her father had turned to alcohol to handle his sorrows, then to a much younger woman, much to her and Keith's disgust. She had tried so hard to stay in Keith's life, refusing to let him go too, even when she knew that he had nothing to do with the rest of the family.

Then, when Keith had joined the military, she'd moved out of her father's house into Keith's place. Maybe to be closer to him. And that helped distance her from the rough homelife of her father's new family, where she was not accepted once more, where she didn't belong either. And it was hard to look back to all those long-ago years and realize how much of that little girl still remained inside Robin and how much these memories triggered her right now because she'd felt *less than good enough* way back then and still felt the same way right now.

It was all so stupid.

She sighed, leaned back, and said, "I wonder if we ever grow up fully." Because really, she wasn't sure that there was any such thing. It's like people took steps forward and then fell back into old childhood patterns. She was thinking she was doing okay but had a few things to deal with, and look at what popped out.

But now she felt more at peace inside. She wasn't done yet, but she was getting there.

She let out a big sigh. This wasn't about Iain. She had never been jealous of his successes. Not in any way. She just wanted to be the best Robin she could be for a worthy man who was giving his all to be the best Iain he could be. He deserved no less. And she now knew that she was plenty good enough for him. She smiled as the tears gathered.

This was the tough part, facing down her demons. The rest is easier. Just look at Iain. She wiped away her tears, but her smile remained.

She put down the journal, threw back the last of her sparkling water, and walked out for dinner. And realized it was almost the end of the dinner hour. She shook her head in surprise and quickened her pace.

As soon as she got to the cafeteria, Dennis raised his eyebrows. "And here I thought you'd be with Iain."

"I was delayed," she explained. She looked at the little bit of food left. Most people had eaten and were now sitting and talking. "Wow," she said. "Did all those horse people from the weekend come back here and clean us out?"

"Not sure what's going on," he said, "but a lot of people were here today."

"I hadn't even realized what time it was," she said. "I've just been so busy." She looked at the food in front of her and said, "Oh my, was it fish and chips today?"

"Well, the chips are looking a little less than perfect right now," he said, "but this is a fresh batch of fish."

She immediately held out her plate and said, "Any coleslaw to go with that?"

He smiled and gave her a big dollop of it. "What else?"

She shook her head. "This might be enough." She walked to the side, dumped vinegar all over her fish, picked up a fork and knife, and headed out to the shade. She wanted to be alone today. She wanted to be away from everyone. She could feel eyes on her, and she didn't know if it was Iain or Dani or someone else. But, for the first time, she understood the need to be alone and the need to just exist without having to give an explanation of what had gone on. It was amazing just what silence of the mind could do. It felt right. By the time she had eaten her fish and coleslaw, she pushed her plate back to the side. It was good, but she'd had enough.

Almost immediately Dennis was there, and he scooped up the empty plate and asked, "More?"

She shook her head. "No, that was wonderful." Then she

looked at his hand and asked, "What is that?"

"Pineapple cheesecake," he said with a fat smile, and he put it down in front of her.

She stared at it, looked at him, and said, "What if I'm dieting?"

"It's a small piece, but I can take it away if you want," he said. Almost instantly the plate disappeared.

"No, no, no," she protested. He chuckled and put it back down, and he disappeared instead. She stared at the dessert, wondering how he could have known that cheesecake was one of her favorites. When he returned a few minutes later with a small china teapot and a cup, she realized just how much he noticed about people. She said, "You'll make me cry."

"No," he said. "No crying. I've already had a lot of that. But if you want a hug ..."

Immediately she bounced to her feet, and he reached out and gave her a gentle hug.

"Don't know what's bothering you today," he said, "but tomorrow is a whole new day."

She smiled, feeling the tears in the corner of her eyes, and she nodded. "It is indeed," she said. "And I hadn't realized just how much I need that tomorrow to come."

"It'll all be okay," he said. "I hope it's not anything wrong with you and Iain?"

She shook her head. "As far as I know, it isn't," she said. "Just some other stupid stuff."

"It's always stupid stuff," he said. "When you break it all apart and take a look at the little bits and pieces, you'd be surprised at just how much stupid stuff it really is."

Seated again, she realized how innocent-sounding and yet how very important Dennis's words were because all this in her mind had built up to something *huge*, and yet it really wasn't. Even feeling that *hugeness*, what she heard from Dennis was something about how she could break it down into smaller bites and deal with it. And she was grateful, not for his intervention, but for his final words to help her put some of this to rest.

When she poured her cup of tea, a shadow fell across her face. She didn't even have to look up to know. "There you are," she said in a teasing voice.

"I wondered if you wanted to be alone," he said quietly.

"I did," she said with a nod. "So, thank you for that. But I'm okay now." He looked at her with worry on his face. She smiled, seeing the gentle giant for who he was. A man, as Dani had said, with a good heart. "Just some troubling thoughts."

"Anything I can help with?"

"No," she said with a shake. "Just a few things I needed to work out for myself."

"And you're good?"

"I'm good," she said. "Look what Dennis brought me."

He stared down on the cheesecake, then looked over at Dennis. "How come you got cheesecake?" he protested, his voice ever-so-slightly louder.

"Well, if you ask him nicely, he might bring you a piece."

"Nah," he said. "I think he saves the best pieces for the girls."

"That's such a sexist remark," she said, chuckling.

"But you know it's true," he said. Yet his grin was wide and infectious.

She smiled at him. "I really am grateful that you came here to Hathaway House."

He stared at her in astonishment, and his smile fell away. He reached across and grabbed her hand. "That's the nicest thing anybody has said to me," he said, his gaze focused on her.

She squeezed his fingers, then dug her fork into the cheesecake, held it up, and said, "You want the first bite?"

He looked at it, looked at her regretfully, then shook his head and said, "No, it's yours. Go ahead."

"But the thing about me is," she said, "I can see a treat like this and realize that two people can enjoy it." And so, she held the first bite out once more. Obediently he opened his mouth, and she popped it in. He closed his eyes, and a happy sigh escaped.

"I do love cheesecake," he muttered.

She chuckled, and they shared the small piece between them, like a special treat. When it was gone, she put the plate off to the side, fork on top, and slowly drew her tea closer. They were still holding hands, something that she really enjoyed. She looked at his thumb, seeing the calluses of a working man's hand versus hers, which were usually kept in very good repair, except for scratches from various animals. She hated to wear gloves, and she always felt that the animals needed the skin-to-skin contact to help calm them down.

"So, what was causing you all that trouble?"

"Just realizing," she said, "that it's okay for somebody to do really well and for the other one to do not so well and then have the roles reversed. It's okay to be jealous for a little bit, and it's okay to acknowledge that jealousy was really something else and then to step past it." She looked at him and smiled. "See? Big thoughts."

He squeezed her fingers and slowly slid his hand away. "You know something? That's one of the things that I was thinking about. Not the same thing, but I heard from Badger."

Her eyebrows rose. "What did he have to say?" She leaned in eagerly.

"He thought that setting up a center like he had done was a perfect idea," he said slowly. "He even had a couple suggestions of who to contact here locally and also contacts about possible grant money." He looked at her a little dazed. "I really didn't expect that."

"And yet I think that's what Badger does, isn't it? And if he can help you help a dozen others, then his job has just multiplied with even greater benefits."

He smiled, nodded, and said, "It's still early yet though. I need months more here."

"And I'm glad to share this time with you while you are here," she said, "because you'll get what you need to fully heal and because I really enjoy having dinner together."

"So, maybe dinner on a long-term basis?"

She looked up at him and could feel a flush rising on her cheeks. "I'm game," she said, tilting her head. "What about you?"

"There's a lot about life that I could face alone, but I would much prefer to have someone at my side. Someone who's *you*."

"Knowing that you can face it alone," she said, with a knowing smile, "allows you the freedom to not have to."

"Exactly," he said. "I'm not 100 percent by any means."

"You're right," she said. "You're more than 100 percent. You had been knocked back about 30 percent, then picked yourself up, and moved forward at such a fast pace to exceed 100 percent. So I know you're well past where you were when you first came in here."

He looked at her, smiled, lifted her fingers, and kissed the tips. "That's one way of looking at it. I think you're biased though."

"It's the best way to look at it," she said. "I couldn't care less about your legs, the one missing a foot or the one that's being strengthened right now. I know your history comes with baggage, and apparently mine does too." And she chuckled. "It's all about tomorrow and every other tomorrow ahead of us."

"I do have some friends in town," he said. "I think I mentioned Bruce to you."

"Yes, and?"

"He's coming by for a visit next weekend," he said. "I'd really like you to meet him. I've told him so much about you."

"You did call him back?"

"I did, and I sent him the pictures that Dani had taken. At that point in time, Bruce wouldn't take any more no-talking from me," he said, laughing. "He knows me too well. I'm starting to feel whole again. I think that's what all this means. I'm starting to feel balanced and grounded, with a real future before me."

"As long as that future," she said, "involves me in some way, then I'm perfectly okay for that to happen."

"I was hoping you'd say that," he said gently. "And, if you were any closer," he said, "I'd attempt to kiss you, but we do have a table between us."

Instantly she got up and walked around the table to sit in his lap.

He burst out laughing at her spontaneity.

She chuckled, leaned over, and whispered, "Did you mean it?"

"Oh, I meant it," he said. "Will you be part of my future? Will you be part of my life? You're already part of my heart, and my soul already knows where you belong."

She nodded and smiled, then gently stroked his lips and said, "My soul knows too."

He reached up, and she leaned down. And when their lips aligned, it was like a promise coming true. When she lifted her head, she heard cheers from everybody around them. She looked out in astonishment, the whole cafeteria full of people listening and watching them. She reached up to clap a hand to her red cheeks, but Dennis just chuckled. He came over with a huge piece of cheesecake for both of them to share in the celebration and said, "That's what we like to see. Happy endings."

Epilogue

JADEN HANCOCK STARED at the email from his buddy. He typed in a quick response. **Is this for real, or are you just full of crap?** He sent it back just as fast. He watched and waited until he got a reply. Iain had been at Hathaway House for several months now. Jaden had heard a few intermittent responses but nothing major, until this one where Iain said he was a new man, and his life was great. If there was any way Jaden could make it happen, he should be coming to Hathaway House too. But, instead of an email coming in, his phone buzzed. He stared at it in surprise and said, "Iain, is that you?"

"It is," said the boisterous voice of his old friend. "And, no, I'm not full of shit. I've done a tremendous amount of growth and improvement here. Coming to Hathaway House was the best thing I could have done."

"Just because it was good for you doesn't mean I should do it," Jaden said cautiously. "I don't travel well."

"Then don't take a truck, like I did," Iain urged immediately. "You know how I felt about that. It was the worst mistake ever. It put me back weeks."

"Well, I don't have a whole lot of choice," he said. "I'm not sure exactly how I would get there, but just traveling alone would probably kill my back."

"And I also know that you think this is as far as you can

go and that you've already adapted and that you've already moved on, so why bother? I'm here to tell you that you can go a whole lot further physically."

"Says you," Jaden scoffed.

"Absolutely, I say so. I've got a call in to Lance too because I think both of you in particular could do well here."

"Maybe. But just the thought of having new medical staff and of starting all over again, trying to explain the problems, the difficulties, and the pain …"

"I get it," Iain said. "I really do. I just don't want you to shortchange what could be much improved on a physical level. I'll send you some photos here in a minute. Of course they're not terribly pretty, but they show the progress on my leg. And it exceeds the progress we were told to expect."

"Sure, but you had surgery. You've had lots of improvements. You're as good as you'll get."

"No, that's the mentality from where you're at," Iain said quietly. "I'm at a much further place."

"So, does that mean you're done with rehab now?"

"No, not quite," Iain said, "but I can see the end in sight."

"You certainly sound different," Jaden said with a frown. His buddy really did sound good, healthy, happy. He sounded like he was a completely new person. "What brought that about?"

"A lot of things," Iain admitted. "A partner for one. My physical health back for another. My future. All of those things are dead important."

"Did you land a partner?" Jaden sagged in his wheelchair in a daze. "I thought you figured that would never happen?"

"And I figured wrong," Iain said firmly. "Along with my mind-set, I needed to shift a lot. And sometimes, when you're stuck in the same place, you just don't see how different some other place can be."

"It's not so bad here."

"You want to stay there?"

"No," Jaden said, looking around. "It's pretty crowded, and it's starting to look like we're all the same."

"So come here," Iain urged. "Try something different."

"How different?" Jaden asked. He stared down at his hands and wondered what happened to the big, stalwart, and strapping young man he'd been, up for any new adventure possible. Ever since he'd been injured, his world had coalesced into this little tiny circle around him.

In a way, it was how he liked it. It was safe. The thought of moving to a new state, moving to a whole new medical team where he'd have to be reinterviewed and reexamined and poked and prodded all over again was enough to make the bile rise up the back of his throat and to give an instinctive and immediate *no* to the plan. But he also knew that Iain had been in a very similar position as Jaden. And, if Iain had had progress, what were the chances of progress for Jaden?

Then he shook his head. No, there wouldn't be any because this was definitely a case of there was no more progress available for Jaden. He'd already become as good as he could get. He wouldn't get any better, even if here—or there—a little bit longer.

While he listened, Iain talked about the food and the pool and the people and the animals. Jaden was more than a little shocked. When he finally put down the phone at the end of their conversation, Jaden stared out the window. He was sitting in a large lounge, and about twelve of them were watching a football game on TV. All of their wheelchairs were lined up, like geriatric patients. People had gotten into the same mind-set here, and that's what he understood now that Iain had seen for himself in places like this.

Jaden had become part of the norm, and that norm became his reality, and anything else looked scary and different and impossible to achieve. He wheeled himself back ever-so-slightly, trying to distance himself a little bit, to see just what was possible.

When his phone buzzed again, he looked down to see images of Iain's leg—the original leg, which he'd certainly seen right after his buddy's surgery. That hamburger blue-black and red gross-looking thing was supposed to be a leg, and then several more photos popped up, showing the improvements. Jaden stared in surprise. Of course his own leg would heal naturally anyway, and it would look a whole lot better with time, even if he stayed here. But when he got to the next picture of Iain's leg, where it showed a strong and fit, heavily muscled leg, followed then by the picture of Iain himself standing on a prosthetic, with no wheelchair or crutches, and a beautiful woman at his side, Jaden's heart lurched.

Crap, he badly wanted something like that for himself. His one good leg was okay. As for his other leg, the doctors had managed to save it, but it was a facsimile of the hamburger that Iain had started with. But just to think that maybe Jaden wouldn't need crutches or a wheelchair down the road? That would be incredible.

He stared at the wheelchair in the first picture of Iain's leg for a long moment. And then, with determination, Jaden headed back to his room. Somewhere had to be an application online or a phone number that he could call and see about getting in that same center. He sent his buddy a text.

Put in a good word for me, he said. **If there's a space, I really want my name on that next available bed.**

It's as good as done came back the instant response. **Now, phone them, and then send in your application with whatever medical crap they need. You won't regret it. I can promise you that.**

This concludes Book 9 of Hathaway House: Iain.

Read about Jaden: Hathaway House, Book 10

Hathaway House: Jaden (Book #10)

Welcome to Hathaway House. Rehab Center. Safe Haven. Second chance at life and love.

Jaden Hancock knows that things could be a lot worse. He still has two arms and two legs, even if one of his legs is so badly damaged it's virtually useless. And it's not that he isn't willing to work toward recovery—it's just hard to see the lack of progress even after weeks of therapy. While he knows that he needs to accept the current state of his body, that acceptance feels like giving up. And he's not prepared to do that.

Brianna Kole crossed the country to get away from her old life. As the newest member of the staff at Hathaway House, she's polite but not overly friendly. The last thing she wants is to get attached and to risk getting hurt again. But, in spite of her reservations, she and Jaden gravitate to each other as the two newcomers to the facility. After that, it isn't long before Brianna's questioning her feelings … and his.

Find Book 10 here!
To find out more visit Dale Mayer's website.
http://smarturl.it/DMSJaden

Author's Note

Thank you for reading Iain: Hathaway House, Book 9! If you enjoyed the book, please take a moment and leave a short review.

Dear reader,

I love to hear from readers, and you can contact me at my website: www.dalemayer.com or at my Facebook author page. To be informed of new releases and special offers, sign up for my newsletter or follow me on BookBub. And if you are interested in joining Dale Mayer's Reader Group, here is the Facebook sign up page.
https://smarturl.it/DaleMayerFBGroup

Cheers,
Dale Mayer

Get THREE Free Books Now!

Have you met the SEALS of Honor?

SEALs of Honor Books 1, 2, and 3. Follow the stories of brave, badass warriors who serve their country with honor and love their women to the limits of life and death.

Read Mason, Hawk, and Dane right now for FREE.

Go here and tell me where to send them!
http://smarturl.it/EthanBofB

About the Author

Dale Mayer is a USA Today bestselling author best known for her Psychic Visions and Family Blood Ties series. Her contemporary romances are raw and full of passion and emotion (Second Chances, SKIN), her thrillers will keep you guessing (By Death series), and her romantic comedies will keep you giggling (It's a Dog's Life and Charmin Marvin Romantic Comedy series).

She honors the stories that come to her – and some of them are crazy and break all the rules and cross multiple genres!

To go with her fiction, she also writes nonfiction in many different fields with books available on resume writing, companion gardening and the US mortgage system. She has recently published her Career Essentials Series. All her books are available in print and ebook format.

Connect with Dale Mayer Online

Dale's Website – www.dalemayer.com
Facebook Personal – https://smarturl.it/DaleMayer
Instagram – https://smarturl.it/DaleMayerInstagram
BookBub – https://smarturl.it/DaleMayerBookbub
Facebook Fan Page – https://smarturl.it/DaleMayerFBFanPage
Goodreads – https://smarturl.it/DaleMayerGoodreads

Also by Dale Mayer

Published Adult Books:

Hathaway House
Aaron, Book 1
Brock, Book 2
Cole, Book 3
Denton, Book 4
Elliot, Book 5
Finn, Book 6
Gregory, Book 7
Heath, Book 8
Iain, Book 9
Jaden, Book 10

The K9 Files
Ethan, Book 1
Pierce, Book 2
Zane, Book 3
Blaze, Book 4
Lucas, Book 5
Parker, Book 6
Carter, Book 7
Weston, Book 8

Lovely Lethal Gardens
Arsenic in the Azaleas, Book 1
Bones in the Begonias, Book 2

Corpse in the Carnations, Book 3
Daggers in the Dahlias, Book 4
Evidence in the Echinacea, Book 5
Footprints in the Ferns, Book 6
Gun in the Gardenias, Book 7
Handcuffs in the Heather, Book 8
Ice Pick in the Ivy, Book 9

Psychic Vision Series
Tuesday's Child
Hide 'n Go Seek
Maddy's Floor
Garden of Sorrow
Knock Knock...
Rare Find
Eyes to the Soul
Now You See Her
Shattered
Into the Abyss
Seeds of Malice
Eye of the Falcon
Itsy-Bitsy Spider
Unmasked
Deep Beneath
From the Ashes
Stroke of Death
Psychic Visions Books 1–3
Psychic Visions Books 4–6
Psychic Visions Books 7–9

By Death Series
Touched by Death
Haunted by Death

Chilled by Death
By Death Books 1–3

Broken Protocols – Romantic Comedy Series
Cat's Meow
Cat's Pajamas
Cat's Cradle
Cat's Claus
Broken Protocols 1-4

Broken and... Mending
Skin
Scars
Scales (of Justice)
Broken but… Mending 1-3

Glory
Genesis
Tori
Celeste
Glory Trilogy

Biker Blues
Morgan: Biker Blues, Volume 1
Cash: Biker Blues, Volume 2

SEALs of Honor
Mason: SEALs of Honor, Book 1
Hawk: SEALs of Honor, Book 2
Dane: SEALs of Honor, Book 3
Swede: SEALs of Honor, Book 4
Shadow: SEALs of Honor, Book 5
Cooper: SEALs of Honor, Book 6

Markus: SEALs of Honor, Book 7

Evan: SEALs of Honor, Book 8

Mason's Wish: SEALs of Honor, Book 9

Chase: SEALs of Honor, Book 10

Brett: SEALs of Honor, Book 11

Devlin: SEALs of Honor, Book 12

Easton: SEALs of Honor, Book 13

Ryder: SEALs of Honor, Book 14

Macklin: SEALs of Honor, Book 15

Corey: SEALs of Honor, Book 16

Warrick: SEALs of Honor, Book 17

Tanner: SEALs of Honor, Book 18

Jackson: SEALs of Honor, Book 19

Kanen: SEALs of Honor, Book 20

Nelson: SEALs of Honor, Book 21

Taylor: SEALs of Honor, Book 22

Colton: SEALs of Honor, Book 23

Troy: SEALs of Honor, Book 24

SEALs of Honor, Books 1–3

SEALs of Honor, Books 4–6

SEALs of Honor, Books 7–10

SEALs of Honor, Books 11–13

SEALs of Honor, Books 14–16

SEALs of Honor, Books 17–19

Heroes for Hire

Levi's Legend: Heroes for Hire, Book 1

Stone's Surrender: Heroes for Hire, Book 2

Merk's Mistake: Heroes for Hire, Book 3

Rhodes's Reward: Heroes for Hire, Book 4

Flynn's Firecracker: Heroes for Hire, Book 5

Logan's Light: Heroes for Hire, Book 6

Harrison's Heart: Heroes for Hire, Book 7
Saul's Sweetheart: Heroes for Hire, Book 8
Dakota's Delight: Heroes for Hire, Book 9
Michael's Mercy (Part of Sleeper SEAL Series)
Tyson's Treasure: Heroes for Hire, Book 10
Jace's Jewel: Heroes for Hire, Book 11
Rory's Rose: Heroes for Hire, Book 12
Brandon's Bliss: Heroes for Hire, Book 13
Liam's Lily: Heroes for Hire, Book 14
North's Nikki: Heroes for Hire, Book 15
Anders's Angel: Heroes for Hire, Book 16
Reyes's Raina: Heroes for Hire, Book 17
Dezi's Diamond: Heroes for Hire, Book 18
Vince's Vixen: Heroes for Hire, Book 19
Ice's Icing: Heroes for Hire, Book 20
Johan's Joy: Heroes for Hire, Book 21
Heroes for Hire, Books 1–3
Heroes for Hire, Books 4–6
Heroes for Hire, Books 7–9
Heroes for Hire, Books 10–12
Heroes for Hire, Books 13–15

SEALs of Steel
Badger: SEALs of Steel, Book 1
Erick: SEALs of Steel, Book 2
Cade: SEALs of Steel, Book 3
Talon: SEALs of Steel, Book 4
Laszlo: SEALs of Steel, Book 5
Geir: SEALs of Steel, Book 6
Jager: SEALs of Steel, Book 7
The Final Reveal: SEALs of Steel, Book 8
SEALs of Steel, Books 1–4

SEALs of Steel, Books 5–8
SEALs of Steel, Books 1–8

The Mavericks
Kerrick, Book 1
Griffin, Book 2
Jax, Book 3
Beau, Book 4
Asher, Book 5
Ryker, Book 6
Miles, Book 7
Nico, Book 8
Keane, Book 9
Lennox, Book 10
Gavin, Book 11
Shane, Book 12

Bullard's Battle Series
Ryland's Reach, Book 1
Cain's Cross, Book 2
Eton's Escape, Book 3
Garret's Gambit, Book 4
Kano's Keep, Book 5
Fallon's Flaw, Book 6
Quinn's Quest, Book 7
Bullard's Beauty, Book 8

Collections
Dare to Be You...
Dare to Love...
Dare to be Strong...
RomanceX3

Standalone Novellas
It's a Dog's Life
Riana's Revenge
Second Chances

Published Young Adult Books:

Family Blood Ties Series
Vampire in Denial
Vampire in Distress
Vampire in Design
Vampire in Deceit
Vampire in Defiance
Vampire in Conflict
Vampire in Chaos
Vampire in Crisis
Vampire in Control
Vampire in Charge
Family Blood Ties Set 1–3
Family Blood Ties Set 1–5
Family Blood Ties Set 4–6
Family Blood Ties Set 7–9
Sian's Solution, A Family Blood Ties Series Prequel
    Novelette

Design series
Dangerous Designs
Deadly Designs
Darkest Designs
Design Series Trilogy

Standalone
In Cassie's Corner